The First Five-Dozen Tales
of Razia Shah
and Other Stories

Cover design by Emir Oručević
Author photo by V. Elisabeth Westwood.

ISBN: 9781695025226

The First Five-Dozen Tales of Razia Shah

and Other Stories

by James Goldberg

Beant Kaur Books
American Fork, Utah

CONTENTS

Introduction

It is a hard world we live in. Not comparatively, I suppose: from Mercury's burning dayside and the sulfuric acid clouds of Venus to the methane lakes of Titan and the incomprehensible cold of the Kuiper belt, there's not a better neighborhood in the system. But from a purely subjective, experiential perspective: yes, it's a hard world.

It was a hard world for our primordial ancestors as they made their way out of fertile oceans to carve out their own niches in blossoming new tenuous ecologies. It was a hard world the first humans faced with an exceptional primate cleverness, developed to dizzying heights by generation after generation of mothers willing to hold us in their wombs while we grew large heads, willing to give hard birth to still-useless young and tend us toward maturity. It was a hard world when we left the niches we'd been nourished in as radically adaptive generalists, guided by aunts' and uncles' and grandparents' commitment to passing on lore to bridge the gap between our instincts and the diverse demands of new environments.

The physical hardships faced by those early humans remain written on bones which we their heirs study from the fantastical comfort of air-conditioned labs, supported by an interdependent population of billions. Our success as a species has been phenomenal, if hardly enough to move me from the claim that it is a hard world we live in. A hard world despite—and perhaps also sometimes because of—all our advances.

Yes, it is a hard world we live in. We no longer face the demands only of members of our own narrow hunter-gatherer bands but must somehow navigate conflicting streams of ideas and expectations that ricochet through a web of media wrapped around the planet. We live in an age of lightning-fast movement and are left to make homes away from home

1

without generations of gradual migration to help us acclimatize. We live in an era of rapid, radical change, with the demands of our age straining the adaptive strength of the lore and culture our families work so hard to let us inherit.

I do not wish to sound ungrateful for plumbing or grocery stores or the wonders of streaming television. But I wonder if the world we live in is *harder* than the one our ancestors knew, because they faced mostly challenges they'd been genetically and culturally prepared for, while many of the challenges we face remain shockingly novel by the standards of our species' history.

We are simply not built for the stresses placed upon us. Simply not built for them.

And what is left for us to do but reach out in search of stories to hold onto as we grope forward through the dark?

James Goldberg
19 July 2019

THE FIRST FIVE-DOZEN TALES OF RAZIA SHAH

THERE'S an apartment in New Delhi, not far from the airport. It's just past the large landfill where Bhuvan the cow wanders free, around the corner from the sweatshop run by Malka the Shrill, and it happens to be where a young woman named Razia Shah lives.

Razia of the incredible intellect, Razia of the thousand-and-one gifts. Razia, who at the age of seventeen is already not sure life is worth living and has thought about a dozen different ways to extinguish the light in her eyes. Razia, who must tell herself a new story each day to convince herself to continue to the next.

It begins one week when the city is being strangled with smog, and the sky is a palpable gray.

1.

Once there as a frog. The frog lived in the bottom of a dry well and spent his days watching the flies far above, waiting only for one to fall dead in the very moment it flew above his home so that he could feast on its corpse. It was a sad existence, but it was his existence, and the frog was careful not to wish for more—until the monsoon season came.

When it rained, the frog no longer lived at the bottom of a dry well, but rather in a narrow, shadowy approximation of what might have been called a pond. And when it rained very

3

hard, the water rose, and then the frog forgot all about the bottom of the well and floated up, up, up until he could go out and see the big wide very wet world.

And here is the moral at the outset of this story: to a frog who lives his life in shadow, even a rainy gray day is a revelation.

Well, as you know, revelation is a dangerous thing. Each time it rained, the frog was tempted further out from the well. At first, he ventured only as far as his frog eyes could see back when he turned his fat head and looked over his ugly frog shoulder. But a frog can only be content with the view over its own ugly shoulder for so long. Soon the frog ventured further, drawn to the tumult of sound and the splattering of mud that emanated from a nearby road. And then—for who can be content to wallow in mud when one has been splashed by it?— he ventured farther and still farther, until one day the frog wandered so far that the rain stopped before he turned back.

It so happened that the sun still shone down on the city, and as the frog blinked about, disoriented by the brightness of a decently lit world, unbeknownst to the frog, the well waters drained and dropped lower. And lower. They receded so far, in fact—and let this be a lesson to you—that the frog might have harmed himself seriously on the jump back down, down, down toward the well's stone floor.

But it didn't really matter—and in that, perhaps, is a moral, too—because on his way home after the storm, the frog was run over by a rickshaw.

2.

High in the mountains, there grew a gnarled tree, and woven into its twisted branches there was a nest, and in that nest sat a bird with three eyes and a magical shadow. From its perch in the nest on the tree in the mountains, the bird would look down down down on the earth with its first two eyes and think "oye, but it is rainy down there."

After all—and let this be a moral—a flood below is a curiosity above.

When it became sunny again, the bird would open its third eye, and look down down down on the world, and see all kinds of things. Things that are hidden from the eyes of mortals and the like of them is told only in stories, sights such as are witnessed only by those once touched by the grace of the bird's shadow.

For instance: the bird could see down into the hill country into the villages where the kings of the stray dogs live before their subjects abandon them and follow the rivers down into the cities of the great Gangetic Plain. In the cities, of course, most stray dogs have four legs. But they must beg for their food as they travel, so along the roadways out of the hills most dogs only have three legs. And when the hills grow steep and uneven, the dogs have only two legs to balance, as befits the land. But few women or men have seen the holy lands of stray dogs where dog-saints balance on a single leg, turning and turning to look every which way for their lost tails.

And none but the bird have seen the land where each of their legless kings dwell, motionless but nonetheless howling terribly and barking out the most vicious threats at its peers, for each king wishes nothing more than to keep each of the other kings from invading its territory. And let this be a moral: he who learns to howl, will always find a reason for howling.

Sometimes, even in the cities, men hear those kings of dogs howling in the distance—but they mistake the terrible, distant sounds for a panic in their own hearts.

5

3.

It happened once (or will happen, or always happens) that a stranger wandered out of the labyrinth where she lived and into the wide and terrible world. First she made her way across fields littered with the plastic ruins of some forgotten civilization, then she followed a river against its own sluggish current until it split into a hundred shallow brooks, then she climbed over mountains that had lost their majestic snow caps and grown bald in the withering heat. On the far side of the mountains, so far from her home that the cords of memory stretched thin, she saw the gleaming towers of a distant city shining weakly through the thick and noxious fog.

When she came closer, she could hear the city, too: the low drone of traffic and the whining melody of roadside altercations, the bartering chatter of commerce and—almost lost in the mix of it all—the occasional whimper or shriek of a child in pain.

As she drew closer to the city, it struck the stranger as strange that for all the commotion within the walls, no travelers had passed her on the road without, along her way. This unnerved her, but it had been so long since she had been in the company of other human beings that the blind need of loneliness pressed her on when wisdom might have stopped her. At length she came to the gate, where she saw someone at last: a man manning a guard station, his face buried in a book.

"Peace to you," she said to the gatekeeper.

"And to you," he replied, looking up from its pages. "On behalf of the year's Sovereign, I bid you welcome to our wondrous city."

"What makes the city wondrous?" the stranger asked.

The gatekeeper set his book aside and studied her. "This is a city where men and women have shrugged off the shackles of fate and choose their own course," he said. "Our freedom is our strength, and our power lies in the potential of each man, woman, and child."

Curiosity and caution warred within the stranger. "Why is it," she asked, "that I passed no traveler on my way?"

The gatekeeper laughed. "Through the Waste Gate? The Sovereign may have placed me here to keep watch for strangers such as yourself, but what that way is worth a journey?" He shook his head. "In this city," he added with a gleam in his eye, "everyone travels the Royal Road." And once again he opened up his book.

"What is the Royal Road?" the stranger asked.

"If you would know our ways," the gatekeeper replied, "the city lies before you."

4.

Once there was a story that had grown gnarled like a geriatric tree on the jagged slopes of an endless mountain. And in that story, as is now widely known, there was a bird with three eyes and a magical shadow.

From its perch on a woven nest in the twisted branches of the gnarled tree on the jagged slopes of the endless mountain, the magical bird can see down the heart of cities into dusty quarters all but invisible to women and men. In one such quarter of Mumbai, there stands a crooked concrete tower, built to scrape the heavens but abandoned and forgotten at the end of a financial crisis, and known only to a tribe of squatters who years ago left its lower levels and migrated into its heights.

On the thirtieth through the forty-first floors they have erected makeshift homes. On the forty-second through forty-fourth floors, they have established markets, on the forty-fifth and forty-sixth floors are an elaborate complex of shrines, and on the forty-seventh floor is a brothel.

The landlords of slums on the floors numbered in the thirties are named Greed and Opportunity and the slumlord on the forty-first floor calls himself Upward Mobility. Most disputes in the markets are settled by an old man, a veteran of the 1962 war with China who had two fingers frozen off at high elevation and can slip playing cards in and out of his sleeve covertly in the gap between his remaining fingers, both to earn money gambling and to read the future. For disputes the old veteran cannot settle, or for the most heinous of crimes, he delivers offenders upward to the Madam of the Brothel for judgment who, if necessary, has them thrown from the dizzying height.

Once there was a one-handed pick-pocket who would attempt to lighten the pockets of the unwary using only the hook he had obtained as a cheap prosthetic. Unfortunately, it is difficult for most people to remain unwary while a thief is trying to pick their pocket with his hook. In the process, he tore a great many articles of clothing, poked a great many people in the hips or rear ends, and himself grew quite destitute. After he had been caught attempting to rob every inhabitant of the tower's thirtieth through forty-first floors, he was delivered to the veteran, who delivered him to the Madam, who unceremoniously removed his hook and cast it from the forty-eighth floor, where it fell down down down down smashing into the ground at length on the side of a highway next to the body of a dead frog.

5.

What seems subtle from a distance is startling up close. This is the moral not only of this story, but also of the art of storytelling itself.

Inside the Waste Gate, the stranger found her ears assaulted by the cacophony of traffic and the roaring of roadside altercations, the noise of it almost drowning out the desperate shouts of hungry hawkers in the marketplace, which in term quite nearly drowned out the regular cries of children in pain. Her nose was filled the scents of human sweat and animal refuse, of burning fuels and burnt morning milk, of stagnant, putrid waters mixed into mud and splattered by passing wheels across the sides of the city's streets.

Everyone seemed to be in a rush: in the great tangle of vehicles and bodies, people swerved and shoved, kicked and crashed. *Is this the royal road everyone takes?* the stranger asked herself as she was pushed along the way. But as she found herself jostled one way and then another, along broad thoroughfares and into narrow, crowded alleys, she could not find any road that went untraveled. Instead, in the teeming streets of that city, the stranger who had escaped a labyrinth tried not to lose herself.

In the center of the city, she came at last to a district where trees still stood and flowers still flourished in a series of ornate gardens. Beyond the gardens stood a complex of buildings made of polished marble. The building at the heart of the complex boasted a gilded roof, walls decorated with designs made of inlaid stones, and a gentle stream flowing through its center to delight the eyes and cool the air.

The stranger managed to restrain a passerby for a few moments. "Is that the palace?" she asked.

The passerby looked at her in disbelief. "Palace? That ancient word barely has place in our language," he said. "We call it the Light of All Eyes, the Heart of Order, and the Abode of Excellence. But yes, it is the dwelling place of the year's Sovereign—as well as the year's counselors and generals and other members of the year's court."

"And where might I find the Royal Road?" the wandering stranger asked. "Is it near here?"

He looked at her closely. "The Royal Road is all around us. You must be a stranger from a distant country not to have heard of our great Meritocracy before."

"Indeed," the stranger said. "I have come across mountains, and over thick-fogged fields, and out of a labyrinth," she said. "But where this Royal Road may be remains a mystery to me."

"Many roads lead to this district," the passerby began, "but only the Royal Road leads to the Light of All Eyes. Come! Sit! Let me tell you the story."

And so the stranger sat and awaited the promised enlightenment.

6.

When the bird in the nest on the branches of the tree that juts out from the mountain of untold height closes its eyes, the world is about to change. As, some say, the world is always doing, but also, all would agree, in ways worthy of a tale's meager ration of attention for a strain to follow in the cacophony of goings-on that make up this wide world. When the bird closes its right eye, judgment is coming. And when it closes its left eye, mercy is upon some unfortunate soul. When it closes its two lower eyes, it is asleep and when it closes all three eyes, it dreams. And then, when it opens its three eyes and spreads its mighty wings and takes flight, all destiny holds its breath until destiny turns slightly purple.

It happened once that the bird flew from its home: a mile, two miles, three miles over the land, and though its shadow was only the size of a needle's eye, fortune truly smiled upon the tailor whose needle's eye crossed under its shadow, for his needle would thenceforth sew straw into gold—if only the tailor were so fortunate as to be so wonderfully incompetent as to thread his needle with straw instead of thread.

When the bird passes over a one-legged dog, it grows another leg and proceeds down the hill and when the bird passes over a two-legged dog it grows another leg, which leaves it with enough to walk but not too many to keep it from begging, and when the bird passes over a three-legged dog, that is where all the frightening, rabid, ill-tempered stray dogs that wander the streets come from.

It happened once that the bird also flew ten thousand feet over a dead frog, which was instantly revived. The frog hobbled up from the road, leaped back to the well and down down down into it, and could thereafter lure swarms of flies as thick as Delhi's smog into its well simply by croaking a hypnotically melodic croak with which it had been gifted.

The she-frogs found the melodious nature of the croak both exotic and off-putting, but—and let this be a moral to any story—who can resist a frog, repulsive as he may be, who catches so many flies?

7.

A thousand year later there was a lost wanderer in a great desert.

He looked this way, he looked that way, and he saw only rocks and sand and tiny scattered fragments of ruins from a city that had eaten itself alive as far as his nearly sand-blind eyes could see. He walked in no particular direction at all and collapsed--afraid (but also not afraid) that he would weep in despair and that the tears would waste his body's last ounces of liquid and he would die.

In the night, the wanderer dreamed of good things to eat: sweet doughy balls, and cakes with the taste of honey and cardamom seed, and tiny fritters shaped like the tracks lizards leave as they skattle their way across the barren wasteland. In his dream, he kept feeling as if something was missing, something he desperately needed, and that's when he heard it: a hypnotically melodic croak.

The dreaming wanderer left the sweets and walked through the freezing winds of the midnight desert toward the sound until he reached what seemed to be the place. He removed five rocks from their places and then a sixth. As he lifted the sixth rock, off slid three pebbles plink, plink, plink—down down down into the waters of the well and the dreamer woke up and fell on his face and drank desperate thirsty gulps of it until he felt human again.

At length, a hideous frog, ancient and terrible, waddled forth from the magical waters of the hidden well. "I will grant you one wish," the frog croaked. And the man wished the last thousand years of madness could be undone—but he forgot to wish that they would not be repeated afterward.

8.

In the shining square of a bustling city where children's screams can always be heard, a passerby stopped to tell a stranger the story its citizens lived by.

"In ancient times," the passerby said, "power succeeded itself in this city through blood: passed from king to king, or else shed between warlord and warlord. But blood moves in no particular direction, except to flee the crushing force of the heart, so the power of the city progressed in no direction but fled continually from the force of history's heartbeat.

"In time, the people tired of incompetent heirs and insatiable strongmen. Our ancestors rose up and seized the centers of power. And they made a compact that henceforth rule would pass by sharpness of wit rather than sharpness of blade. Each year, they would offer every man, woman, and especially child the chance to prove themselves worthy, through various ingenious tests, to be raised to the rank of

Sovereign for the year, or to secure a place of power and privilege on that year's court. And so it was that our city became famous for opening the path to power—not to mention luxury and fame—wide enough for all to enter.

"We call our preparations to prove ourselves 'The Royal Road,' and with rewards so great, can it be any surprise that so many travel this most distinguished way? If they do not take the way themselves, every family at least sends their children."

The stranger hesitated. She had seen no children on the streets. "How do children take this road if they never seem to leave their homes?" she asked.

But the passerby only laughed. "Who has time to leave home when they still have a chance to study for greatness?" he said. "I only allow myself the waste of a walk through these grounds because the years have proven I have no great talent. But my daughters and sons are young yet, so they take the Royal Road under my wife's attentive eye." The man inclined his ear. "Perhaps you can hear them in the distance even now," he said, "being driven along the road—though only time will tell if they have stumbled along like donkeys or galloped like stallions."

"And if they do not find themselves on the court at that next test?" the stranger asked.

The citizen took in a deep, satisfied breath. "In a city such as this, hope retains its audacity! So long as there is still skin left to beat, we will drive young and old alike toward a better result the next year." He shrugged. "Even one with prospects as poor as mine may still have a chance, if next year I again apply myself to the task." He eyed her. "You, too, could buy yourself books and try your chance. The road may be long but it is also wide!"

But before he could tell her how to begin, the stranger walked away.

9.

In a city of screams, surrounded by smog, the stranger walked. All around her now, through narrow windows, she could see the bowed bodies and bent heads of travelers on an unseen path—travelers seeking glory for their merits or else weeping softly for the shame of their shortcomings.

She found herself dizzy with the sight of lamps in every window as evening fell. Sick with the scent of ash from the lamps where children studied. And as she stumbled through the streets, searching for a gate back out into the wastes, she found the city's grip on her loosening, so that at times she sank down into the ground: first ankles, then waist, then chest losing themselves in the dirt. Other times, as the lightness of the dirt passed around her without holding her fast, she found herself floating up through the dirt and then out into the air, walking higher and higher above the streets as the people below seemed to grow smaller and less significant. And though her own body was close, she too seemed to grow smaller and smaller and less and less important.

Until she didn't matter at all.

Until no one mattered at all and nothing mattered at all. Except perhaps the wind as it grew stiffer and stronger and threatened to blow her forever away.

And away and away and away...

10.

Once upon a time.

Once upon a time there was a girl who could say "once upon a time." And people said she did it to escape—but that wasn't true. She said it to keep herself from escaping.

She said it because once upon a time was an anchor, a fixed point, an x on a map of space and time, while her own world rolled beneath her like the ravenous sea. She said it because it sounded so good to stand on a once—at a single moment when something is going to happen and not always stretched between some hoped-upon-her far-off future and pressures that had been building in the past since before she was born.

Once upon a time there was a girl trapped in a no-man's-land between times, who was trying desperately to spin a somewhere beneath her feet.

11.

Once upon a time there were two orphans, a sister and a brother, whose mother had been the deposed princess of a string of islands that later vanished beneath the rising waves of the ravenous sea. The two traveled together, begging for bread through the day and for shelter by night, until their minds grew weary of this world's roads and they felt they could travel no more. At a crossroads, they decided to separate, each promising to return if the next village proved promising. First the girl turned to the right and the boy to the left, but each soon came back to wish the other another farewell, after which the girl went off to the left and the boy went to the right.

Down the road to the left of the crossroads, the girl found a village more wicked and inhospitable than any the orphans had chanced upon before. In that village, they beat people for begging and they all barred their doors at night and grew enraged if they heard some poor soul make a sound while seeking shelter. She soon learned that this was because of a tiger who often stalked the village by night: the people had no pity for the wandering poor but feared at every noise for their own lives.

The girl soon returned to the crossroads, but her brother was not there. She thought about going down the road to seek him but considered that perhaps he had met a grim fate in a village still worse than the one she had found. So she returned to the wicked village and did her best to survive. The girl soon learned to sleep in the day. In last hour before evening finally became night, she would sneak out into the forest and look for the tracks of the tiger, then follow them into the first field they passed through, where she would gather grain the great beast had knocked down when it passed. No one scolded her, for if they had heard a noise and looked out to glimpse the tiger's eyes, they never dared to glance out of the house again until morning.

Let this be a lesson: no one notices a beggar when they fear a tiger.

So long as the tiger did not turn and notice the girl, she could remain nourished and safe. She slept by day, she gathered by night, and once each week, she returned to the crossroads, hoping against hope that her brother still lived.

12.

Meanwhile, down the road to the right of the crossroads, the boy found a village that was clean and well ordered, where the people offered him food before he had the chance to ask. He soon learned that their headman was dying, and that the council of five who led the village were eager to see acts of charity performed, in the hopes that their goodness would be rewarded with the headman's recovery. Soon the headman died, but all the people of the village concluded that the wandering orphan had been sent by God to replace the wisdom of their beloved leader, who had once himself come to the village as a wandering orphan. They gave him a house and fed him fresh bread and yogurt each morning, but though the boy wished to return to the crossroads to tell his sister of his good fortune, the people begged him to stay. And, because they had been kind to him as a beggar, he could hardly reject their pleading.

And so the boy stayed and became a worthy heir of his noble predecessor. He resolved disputes in a spirit of wisdom and equity. He offered the people of the village vision and purpose. And he was generous and unselfish with them, perhaps to a fault, for every time he asked leave to return to the crossroads, they begged him to stay. And as often as they begged, he relented and promised to delay his trip, though doing so weighed heavily on his conscience. Soon he found it difficult to eat the bread and yogurt they offered him, thinking his sister might be hungry, and he found it difficult to sleep in the fine house they'd given him, thinking his sister might be sleeping somewhere in the dirt. He grew thin, haggard with hunger, and his eyes grew bloodshot with the lack of sleep.

13.

Meanwhile, in the forest around the village along the path on the other side of the crossroads, the tiger continued to stalk each night. The tiger knew the villagers well—and answered the greed he smelled in them from the forest each day with fear as he stalked between their homes each night. He had pity on their poor, abused beasts of burden, but would eat a particularly cruel-smelling man from time to time, both to appease his own hunger and to offer them fair warning to turn away from their wickedness.

The tiger noticed, of course, that whenever he crossed his own path, there were light footprints in the center of his own heavy paw prints, their steps twined together like fates written onto the very face of the earth. And whenever the breeze blew, the tiger stopped to marvel at the rare scent of human goodness coming from the girl somewhere on the path behind him.

One night, when the moon was full, the tiger stopped in his path, crouched low, and waited for the girl to come upon him. When she saw him, she gasped, but he spoke to her before she could run. "Do not think I am crouching so that I can pounce and tear you limb from limb," he said. "For I am crouching low not to leap, teeth flashing against the black of the night, but to bow before you." When the girl stayed to listen instead of running, the tiger continued. "I understand," he said, "if you find it hard to trust me, but listen to this lesson: whoever does not fear the tiger's crouch is worthy of his bow."

And the girl stepped closer and touched him gently, so he showed her the way back to his home and asked her to be his wife.

14.

In another village, near a well that had run dry and filled up only in the monsoon season, there lived a girl with an unusual gift. Her knitting needles, having been touched by a bird's magical shadow, could turn old castaway clothes back into the animals whose wool they had been woven from.

Her brothers—for she had many, taken in from here and from there despite her parents' poverty—went from place to place, gathering tattered, unwanted shirts and socks, skullcaps and sweaters. Her mother sorted out the ones that would only turn into piles of plastic and her father sorted out the ones that would produce only cotton plants. The remainder the girl transformed into flocks of sheep and goats, with the occasional camel or alpaca, and once—inexplicably—a woolly mammoth.

The family soon went into business producing yogurt and became quite wealthy. But their animals ate all the grass and the village became little more than a pile of mud until, one fateful monsoon, it all washed away.

15.

There was a cloud once: one with grand aspirations. Its father was a long, thin, stringy cloud and its mother was a soft, puffy, round cloud and both of them wished for nothing more than for their child to take shape as water, to move from their poor neighborhood in the upper reaches of the atmosphere, through the more fashionable neighborhoods with a view of the countryside below, all the way to the ground where the famous rivers dwell with the rich earth.

And the little cloud worked hard and studied long and grew thick with moisture until it fell down down down through the atmosphere with such violence that it tore the face of the land away.

And the cloud wept to think of how hard it had struck the same earth it had once admired from a distance, but its tears only tore more at the rootless ground. So the cloud regretted all it had done, and wished the sun would rise to beat down on it and release it back into the freedom of the air.

16.

There was once a farmer who had worked so hard and so carefully for years, that even God found it a shame to let his work be spoiled and spared his fields from every misfortune that struck his neighbor. The farmer had grown wealthy even as his friends—for he still counted all his neighbor as his closest friends—struggled to eke a living out of the poor, eroded ground.

The farmer felt the burden of his friends' poverty. He offered them work, he offered them charity, but some curse always seemed to stand between them and the land. Year by year, when another family found themselves on brink of starvation and ready to quit the land for good, the farmer took from the wealth he'd earned of years of improbable surplus and bought their dry land for a sum great enough to allow them to start a life elsewhere. And one by one, the other families gladly left the thin, dry earth until only one remained.

One spring, the farmer went to his last neighbor, whose wife was cooking their last sack of flour and their last jar of butter into bread. "My friend," he said, "I need a new well dug, but my back has grown brittle and sore and I hate to dig for myself." He asked his friend to come and dig the well for him.

It was not the first time the farmer's friend had been offered help from the improbably fortunate farmer. But years of deferring to the needs of others had built in him habits so strong he found it almost impossible to accept aid for himself. And so the two always circled each other, the terrible struggle of life in their village at the unspoken center of all their discussions.

And let their stance toward that center be a moral of this story.

Upon hearing the generous sum the farmer intended to pay, the friend initially declined. "That is far too much," he said. But the farmer insisted. "Anyone with a firm back and a pair of hands would gladly do the work for half that amount," the friend advised. Still, the farmer insisted.

At length, the farmer offered a fraction less, and his friend declined more slowly, then another fraction less and his friend declined still more slowly, until at last they haggled their way to an agreement halfway between the farmer's first offer and a standard wage.

Another moral of the story? If something is worth doing, it is worth haggling over.

17.

The sun rose one day to find a man already digging in a field not his own.

The man dug through the morning. The sun, watching, tried to persuade him to rest from his labors, but the man continued to dig through the heat of the day as the sun beat down him.

And though the wife of the farmer who had hired the man called him to come into the house for bread and yogurt, he continued to dig in the evening, long after the sun was no longer there to watch. Digging, after all is labor, and labor, at times, approaches oblivion and oblivion, the ancient sages say, is perhaps worship—or, then again, perhaps worship's ultimate aim.

In any case, the laborer dug and the feel of the shovel against his hands was sweet until he was so lost in his work that he forgot the shovel and forgot the world and forgot even himself until, in the night, the man's shovel struck something hard.

The man, reluctantly, stopped digging and discovered his shovel had struck a box. "This might perhaps belong to the farmer," the laborer thought, and though it was extremely heavy, he carried it inside.

The farmer told his friend the laborer that he had never before seen the box, and after the laborer had eaten, the two agreed to open it and see what lay within. Together, they pried off the lid and found the box stuffed fulled of gems: rubies as large as their fists, a diamond the size of a human heart, precious stones of blue and green and yellow crammed into the crevices between the larger treasures.

Both of them were astounded. "God has blessed you indeed," the laborer said, "to have laid such a treasure beneath your field."

"No, God has blessed you," the farmer insisted. "To have given such a treasure into your hands."

The two argued late into the night, each giving the reasons and evidences why the treasure must have been the other's miracle and why, in consequence, the other should be the possessor of the newfound wealth. But neither could convince the other that he deserved ownership of the jewels. In the morning, their wives cooked flour and butter into breakfast as the two men continued their caravan of explanations and justifications, until at last the laborer's wife said, "Enough! I have heard of a village not far from here where the next headman is always sent by God and renders judgment only according to his wisdom. Go and ask him: only promise to accept his opinion and allow him to settle the matter." The two men each swore to do so and began their journey together toward the village.

18.

Once upon a time, at a certain spot on the slopes of the hill country, there dwelt a stray dog who had left the land of his kind's kings and the land of his kind's saints to stand with his two paws facing downward toward a valley while his legless rear sat contentedly a little higher up, tail wagging like a flag in a show of perpetual canine happiness.

Because he was facing out toward the wide world, the two-legged dog did not see the mudslide behind him—and so he was struck by surprise—not to mention by a camel, with an alpaca on its back—as the remains of a village careened down toward the valley, where dog, camel, alpaca, the crumpled ruins of several houses, battered bits of a yogurt factory, and—inexplicably—a wooly mammoth finally came to mud-covered rest.

For all who hear this story, a moral is easy to discern: if a camel comes packing an alpaca, be aware.

But for the poor dog, whose eyes were covered in mud, the moral was impossible to see.

19.

Once, between times, there was a juggler. And oh, what a juggler—in addition to balls, knives, torches, and boulders, she juggled nightmares. If she had stopped and held any one of them too long, the smoky taste of it would have choked her. But somehow, if she threw them up amid some hopes, plans, aspirations, and whimsy, and kept each moving moving always moving, none could get a firm hold on her.

And so the juggler juggled from the hours before dawn, juggled beneath the burning gaze of the sun through the heat of the day, juggled on even after—especially after—the evening drew to a close and the crowds wandered home, their thirst for novelty satiated, as the nightmares grew most hungry.

She juggled through the night. Moving moving.

Juggling for her life.

20.

There was a girl once who had marriage proposed to her by a tiger. And because the tiger had been kind to her, and because he had taken her into his home when no human had offered her shelter, and because his eyes were bright and his fur soft and his claws strikingly handsome, she considered.

"It may be," she said, "that I will marry you. Only: I am a human—and cannot abide the thought of eating human flesh."

The tiger assured her she did not need to worry. "I will hunt the beasts of the jungle for you," he said, "and scare away the wicked farmers when you gather grain. You will always have enough to eat without me sharing a man with you when I take one."

But the girl was not satisfied. If he would have her for his wife, she insisted, he would have to give up eating her fellow human beings.

"What do you care for them?" the tiger asked, eyes burning. "They were cruel to you!"

The girl cast her eyes down toward the floor. She could not deny the tiger was right. But still, she insisted.

"The humans of that village understand only fear," the tiger said. "How can I speak to them without using their mother tongue?"

The girl gave no answer, but neither did she withdraw her request. And at length, the tiger relented.

"Very well," he said. "Though I fear this will be the cause of some future evil."

And the girl thanked him, and consented to marry him, then prayed that tomorrow's evil would prove a small price to pay for today's good.

21.

Once a prosperous farmer and his friend, the laborer, came to a village blessed perpetually with a bearer of wisdom at its head. "Is it true," they asked, "that your headman can settle even the most perplexing of difficulties?" And the villagers assured him that it was and carried him before an emaciated boy with bloodshot eyes.

Though the sight of the young man startled both the farmer and his friend, they had promised to lay their case before him and proceeded to do so. "While digging on his land," the laborer said, pointing to the farmer, "I found a box: and in that box, a treasure. But he refuses to accept it as his—and insists against all reason that the treasure must belong to me."

The farmer, hearing this, shook his head. "It is true that the box was found beneath the earth I cultivate," he admitted, "but it was found only by the work of his hands. Land belongs not to men but nourishes us while we live and swallows our ashes after we die. But the work of a man's hands exists only so long as he lives to labor, so the treasures belongs not to me but to him."

The laborer objected to this, and the farmer objected to that, and they argued for some time. "If I were to spend the treasure in my lifetime," the laborer said at length, "perhaps my friend would be correct. But the gems are surely older than I and will remain after I am gone. Let them go, as I have said, with the land—for it is their nearest equal in age and their natural companion."

The farmer opened his mouth to reply, but the worn young headman raised a tired arm for silence. "Does this dispute extend beyond your lifetimes, then? Does each of you have children?"

"He has a son!" the laborer said. "Who will be his heir. If he will not accept the treasures for himself, then surely he should be bound to do it for his son's sake."

"My son will inherit my farm," the farmer said. "My friend had, or perhaps has, a daughter."

"Perhaps?" asked the headman.

"She was lost in a storm as a child," the laborer noted, with a melancholy fragrant as aged wine in his voice.

"He has never given up hope she may return," the farmer said, and then, turning to his friend, he added, "And if she does return to the land he has clung to for her sake, she will deserve such a dowry. If you will not take the treasure for yourself, then take it for her!"

But even to this, the laborer would not agree.

"Enough," the young headman said. "If one of you has a son and one of you has a daughter, then let them both be sent—or searched—for. And if they will agree to be married, they can inherit the jewels together."

So the farmer sent for his wife and son and the laborer for his wife and the people of the village went out searching for the lost daughter while the headman charged one trusted adviser to search for fresh lamb and another to obtain the finest yogurt that could be found to prepare a wedding feast.

And soon the farmer's son arrived and the farmer's wife arrived. And later, the laborer's wife arrived and the people of the village returned without any tales of lost orphan girls found in a storm and raised by some generous couple as their own. But the headman's trusted advisers did not return for quite some time.

22.

What makes food fine?

We say a wine is worthy if it is old or hails from a famous vineyard, but perhaps the taste of these stories on our minds makes far more difference than the feel of a precise chemical configuration on the tongue, for when friends drink fine wine, most of the taste they perceive comes, truth be told, not from the wine but from its bottle.

It happened once that two trusted advisers of a village headman renowned for his great wisdom stopped in town after town and shop after shop asking after stories. They heard of sheep so shapely passing poets had begged to compose paeans to their perfection. They heard of sheep with noble pedigrees, sheep with ancestors from the most noted hills and valleys, sheep whose ancient ancestors came from the divine flocks of deities representing the four elements—whose powers would be at their strongest in the intersection represented in the current generation's lamb. They heard of lambs whose mothers had been watered all their lives from purified water poured into silver troughs, who had never once been made to drink from the compromised waters of polluted rivers.

All these they passed by.

They heard of yogurts from the milk of animals no less storied than those lambs. They heard of yogurts based on cultures older than Sanskrit lettering. They heard of yogurts reputed to have cured the most hideous of physical afflictions and relieved the most severe of existential pains.

All these they passed by.

At last, they came upon a mud-covered homeless family followed by a procession of various muddy animals, who shared with them a tale of a bird's fateful shadow, enchanting knitting needles, unforeseen wealth and an ensuing environmental disaster.

The advisers told the muddy family of a coming wedding: the girl with the knitting needles borrowed a horsehair brush and spun a piece of it into a tall white charger for the groom to ride on when the day for the wedding procession came.

The advisers begged her and her family to come with them, bringing their famed hill country yogurt and their motley menagerie with them to the hoped for wedding feast.

23.

There was a girl once. There was a girl, there was a girl. And she tried so hard to believe in the hope she spoke almost into existence each night. Tried each day, as she trudged down the Royal Road, to believe in her power to create, despite everything. To generate warmth in a world locked in the cold hands of entropy.

There was a girl once. There was a girl, there was a girl.

24.

It was late in the evening when a procession of refugees—including one girl, her many brothers, and at least one inexplicable animal—reached a village where they had agreed to help cater a wedding feast.

The girl looked away shyly when she caught sight of the groom. But though she looked and she looked, she could not find the bride.

"Where is she?" she asked at last.

"I do not know," said the bride's mother.

And her voice sounded like terror. Like the love in a long-ago terror the girl could still remember hearing through the dark and the rain.

25.

There was a girl once. There was a girl, there was a girl.

And she tried to remember. She tried to remember a feeling before grey. Before the grey and the rain. The rain coming down hard and thick, tearing at the land. Tearing away all the rootless ground she could have stood on if it were more than slick, barren mud.

She tried to remember a world before the rain tore at the earth, tore at her clothes, tore at her skin and her hair. Tore, when she opened them, at her eyes.

26.

It happened once that a laborer and his wife gathered for their lost daughter's wedding only to find a yogurt vendor bursting into tears. "Mother?" she asked. "Father? Can it be you?"

And when they had washed the mud off her face and saw their own features melded together and reflected back, they could say with complete confidence and the voice of trembling memory that yes, indeed, it was.

They welcomed their daughter with embraces they had held within for years and they welcomed her parents and her brothers as they would their own blood. And then they asked her if she would like to be married and inherit a great sum—and when she had learned of the groom-to-be's father's good-heartedness and tasted the groom-to-be's mother's good cooking, she agreed that with such parents, she would happily take the son, too. And she glanced at the groom just a little less shyly and the whole village gathered to rejoice and to dance and to sing.

The groom rode up on a white charger and the girl was adorned with jewels of yellow, green, and blue, and the groom's people feasted and the bride's people feasted and the villagers feasted.

But their headman, who was the guest of honor, refused to eat at all for worry over a concern he would not disclose, no matter how the father of the bride and the father of the groom begged him.

27.

There was once a man who hated nothing so much as he hated a thief, and in consequence saw everyone and everything as robbing him.

He hated the mice who stole his crumbs, but also the snakes who stole his mice, and even the mongoose who stole his snakes. He hated the tree that stole his water and the fruit that stole sap from his tree, and seeds that hid themselves in the center of his fruit and stole strength from inside. He hated his ox because it always tried to carry away his plow, and the plow because it had a habit of prying up pieces of his dirt.

At night, he hated the earth for turning and stealing his light and at midday he hated the sun for rising and for creeping up step by step until it almost stole away his shadow. He hated his parents for stealing the cot he kept on his roof, hated his wife for stealing half of his bed, hated his children for stealing the quiet from the very air around him.

But most of all, he hated the beggar who stole the fallen grain from his fields and the tiger that sheltered her and stole away his right to exact justice.

One evening, between the robberies of day and night, the man called his wicked neighbors together. "We have been fools," he told them, "to fear the tiger. For we still see his paw prints in our fields in the morning, but when was the last time that overgrown stray killed anyone?"

28.

There once was a cow. Named, perhaps, Bhuvanesh. And everyone honored the cow, and let it roam freely through the landfill and take first pick of the garbage.

But when no one was looking, many of the boys from the nearby school used to go and throw rocks at it. For sport, perhaps. Or for the dark rush of power they felt in any act of desecration.

The boys wandered the landfill in a pack and pelted the cow with rocks, beating and bruising it.

And the girl who passed them every day was too frightened to ask them to stop—and prayed only never, ever to be seen.

29.

It happened one night that the tiger's wife was at home, cooking, waiting for her husband to return, when she heard a strange, and strangely melodic, melody. As soon as her labors permitted, she slipped out to listen—and who should approach her but a hideous old toad, croaking out a riddle?

Every forgotten well is my well, the frog croaked. *Every new rain brings me up to a new world.*

What I am?

The girl who had married the tiger thought and thought, but she could not solve the riddle. "I don't know," she told the frog.

But the frog remained before her. *What am I?* he croaked again. *What am I what am I what am I?*

"I don't know," the girl said.

What am I? the frog croaked again, so mournfully that they both wept.

Then the frog looked down at the pool of their tears and the girl looked down into the pool of their tears and through the pool she saw her brother, emaciated with bloodshot eyes and shaking from a fever.

A short time later she heard her husband the tiger approaching. Which was odd, since he usually stalked through the forest so silently. "Husband," she said, "a toad came to me. And I know what this toad is, for this toad is kind: he has shown me that my brother is alive, but that he is in desperate need and I must go to him."

"Then you must go to him," her husband the tiger said as he dragged himself into their home and collapsed on its floor. But the girl saw that there were long red streaks on his side.

What am I? the frog croaked. *What am I?*

"Oh my husband!" she cried. "What has happened to you?"

"The wicked men of the village no longer fear me," the tiger said, "and so tonight, they gathered together like a pack of dogs and in a great and powerful rush they fell on me and

31

cut me and because I had promised not to eat them, I had to flee back into the forest to escape."

And the girl clung to the fur on the tiger's side. She washed his wounds with her salty tears and bound the wounds on his sides, but his blood soaked through the bandages. "You must go," he growled, "to your brother. Before they track me to this place and avenge their losses on you."

So she helped him to hide and set out to beg help from her dying brother as the frog croaked *what am I?*

30.

Once there was a rainstorm. Great, violent sheets of rain that fell on an overgrazed, eroded hill and swept a village down into a valley before the waters gathered in a torrent and raged down to a river, where they gathered human refuse and the corpses of animals and grew thick with filth before emptying into the sea.

In the sea, the sun beat down upon the waters. And particle after particle, they rose from water to air, and floated up into a cloud, where they gathered, and grew thick and fell again and again against the hillside and into the river and out to the sea.

Again and again and again and again. Always the same, tearing away at the face of the earth, the same in tears of sorrow as in tears of rage.

31.

Once there were two orphans who parted ways at a crossroads. At first the boy turned to the left and the girl to the right, but then they came back to the crossroads to wish each other, once again, farewell, and the boy went to the right while the girl left to the left. And so it was that their fates became tangled: she went to a bad village and found happiness, while he went to a good village and found misery.

She returned to find him as the guest of honor on the second day of a wedding feast, starving to death and shaking with fever.

"Brother," she asked, "what has happened to you?"

He looked at her in disbelief, not sure if she was living or a ghost. "They made me their headman and begged me not to leave," he answered, "and I grew sick with worry at breaking my promise. Oh, sister!" he said. "Forgive me before I die!"

"You will not die," the girl said, "for I have the very means to heal you. My husband lies hidden outside of a wicked village, where all the men wish to kill him. If you could perform an act of charity and rescue him, perhaps God would save you!"

The brother closed his eyes and nodded his head. "Yes," he said. "I see that it must be done."

The villagers begged him not to go. "For," they admitted, "we knew from the beginning that an evil village lies on the other side of the crossroads, and we feared from the beginning that they would kill you."

But the brother, for once, refused their entreaties, and invited the wedding guests to march with him as his troops. And they all consented to come: the groom on his white charger, the bride on a camel, serving as commander over a battalion of sheep and a division of goats, the headman himself riding—inexplicably —atop the back of a woolly mammoth.

Down the road they rode, kicking up a great cloud of dust that was hidden by the cloak of night. When they reached the village on the far side of the crossroads, they learned that its men had ventured into the forest in pursuit of the tiger and they gave them chase.

And they surrounded the men of the evil village, who had surrounded the tiger, who lay, in a heap, surrounded by blood-soaked bandages.

When the leader of the evil men saw that the army was upon him, he cursed the night for hiding away the signs of their approach, and he cursed time for cheating him out of killing the tiger, and he cursed the brother's troops for stealing his great victory.

So the army advanced and the evil men surrendered and the tiger sat in his blood.

"Once again," he said as his wife approached him, "I bow low before you."

And she summoned the muddy bride-general, who used her magic knitting needles to sew his wounds safely shut. And the girl and her husband and her brother—whose fever had miraculously left him—and the wedding guests and the flocks of sheep and herds of goats returned to the good village, where the people welcomed the tiger as their new God-sent headman and gave the brother leave to wander the wide world.

32.

Once upon a time there was a woman who had the power to capture time. She would take magical sand and heat it in a magical fire until it transformed—as magic so often allows things to do—in this case from solid grains to a molten liquid that she could mold and shape by the application of air.

She would blow the molten glass into vessels of different shapes, to catch time and preserve its flavors. And so she collected dusky bottles for nostalgia and clear jars for moments of insight and a deep green container to hold rest she could gift to the weary.

But though she could bottle time, save time, shift time, she never learned the secret of how to reverse time. And so it was that, when she studied the stars of a man she loved and learned he was fated to die, she wept for days and days.

When she had finished weeping, she asked her parents to speak with his and propose a match. The parents agreed, and the man agreed, and a date was set for a wedding seven months later. Just a month before, as the stars had told her, a cancer within would begin to devour him.

She could not reverse time, but she was determined to face it—though she could not say whether to do so was to defeat it or to be defeated by it more fully than death ever defeated anyone.

After the engagement was celebrated, the woman shut herself up in her workshop and worked and worked and worked for months, so that on the day of her wedding, she and the man she loved could stand together in a hall of mirrors.

Magic mirrors. Time-bending mirrors, placed opposite each other.

He was beautiful, on the wedding day. She loved the light in his eyes as they faced each other in that enchanted hall.

And they lived happily ever after happily ever after happily happily ever ever after after after.

33.

In a city built in an abandoned tower, a city even the ground had forgotten, there lived a man with eight fingers and two gaps between his fingers. Those gaps—the legacy of a forgotten war on a faraway field halfway between earth and sky, where not even the air can keep warmth from slipping away between its fingers—were just as useful as if they had been part of his body, except that they also formed a window through which he could sometimes glimpse the future.

In the grey marketplace of his lost city, the man had a shop where he traded in debts. With a little help from the gap between his fingers, he offered new debts to young gamblers looking to initiate themselves into the traditions of their forebearers, and he maintained the stately old debts of gamblers who could not imagine life without such an accessory.

In the evenings, however, he traded debts: traded them as strategically as the seasoned card player—and, it must be admitted, occasional cheater—that he was, using an exchange of the city's many embarrassments to keep it in a state of relative peace.

It happened one night, after the women and the men of the marketplace had come to him with their disputes, their petitions, their cries for justice and their pleas for mercy, that he looked out through the gap left by his lost fingers into his drink, and through his drink into things to come, and saw that the tower which housed his forgotten city would soon be remembered.

And so it was that the very next morning, the man with the missing fingers shuttered his debt shop and deferred all disputes to the Madam of the brothel. He took the journey down forty-three flights of stairs and out into the streets below, determined to stop the ill fate that was about to encroach upon his beloved home.

Moral of the story: a true hero will go to great lengths to keep from being remembered.

34.

There once was a prince, kind-hearted and fair-faced, loved by all his people, who fell ill with some affliction. He could feel some force pressing against him from the inside, a darkness growing gut-deep within. It grew hard for him to eat and hard for him to sleep. His scalp itched and his skin itched: even his lips itched. His eyes grew sunken and yellow.

The king and the queen called for physicians and magicians from near and far, who studied the prince and consulted with the parents. This cure failed and that cure failed. At length, the doctors of arts both arcane and mundane met together in council and agreed that there was only one remaining explanation: a portal to the world of the dead was beginning to open up inside the prince, eager to devour not only his body, but all the land of the living.

They counseled the king and queen about what should be done next. When they heard the doctors' advice, the queen shouted and the king wept, but the prince, who had listened from the next room, agreed it was the only way.

So they locked the prince high up in a tower, far away from the living world. And in the tower, he drank poison each day to fool death into thinking he was already its own.

The poison was thick and bitter: it burned his throat and rotted away the lining of his stomach, but each day the prince thought of the distant world and he drank. He drank, and he retched black vomit, and he lost all the hair on his head, his face, his chest, his arms, his legs. He lost the hair up his nose and the hair of his eyelashes and he sat in the tower and he drank poison alone alone alone.

For a world that was so far away.

35.

There was once a city forged of glass, framed in steel, that rose above a thousand shanty towns. And in a shining tower in that city, there lived a man who dressed in white and black with a tiny splash of silken color hanging down from his neck. The man earned his living by learning to see and to pull on the invisible threads that tie together those who live in the human realms, and each year he grew more skilled at that art, and in consequence more wealthy, than any natural born native of that glass city ever was.

But as his sight and skill grew, it became more and more clear to the man how he, too, was bound by the threads of attachment he pulled. And as his sight grew, it became harder and harder for him to see past the tangled mass of attachment to a physical world beyond, until he became convinced that all is illusion and that we have tethered ourselves to a nothingness.

So the man left his glass tower and set out to sever himself from the invisible threads that bound him, as sure as any chain, to illusion.

He moved at first into a hovel in the slums, but as the rain fell on the thin sheet of his roof, he could see a thread of attachment forming between himself and its simple shelter. So he left that place and lived by the side of a highway, sleeping at night on a rented cot at an open-air hostel, until he saw a thread of attachment forming between himself and the cot. Next he slept on the ground in the public square where men wait to be hired as laborers, and worked carrying the dust to make cement in a bowl on his head, but soon learned that the anticipation of that menial work left him with a thin thread of attachment to the anticipation that flowed each morning through the square's open air when the contractors came.

So he left his work, and let his tattered clothes disintegrate, until his only attachment was to a simple earthen bowl he left out, as indifferently as he could manage, in case some kind soul happened to fill it with food. Each evening, fed or starving, he took the bowl to a nearby stream and drank from its muddy waters. Until one day, he noticed another beggar reaching down and cupping the water in his hands.

Then he threw away the bowl, free of attachment at last.

36.

What am I? a toad asked a goat one day, as the goat grazed on some grass near a well.

The goat looked him up and down before it answered. "Meh," it said.

What am I? the toad asked an old ewe during a rainstorm later, in another part of the country.

The sheep studied him, apparently with great contempt, for "Bah" is how the sheep replied.

What am I? the toad asked a broken, discarded prosthetic hook on another occasion.

And the hook glinted at him knowingly, but it said nothing at all.

37.

In the city of glass, there lived another banker: one with neither the skill to be great nor the connections to seem strong. After a promising youth in the top four-fifths of his class, he was consigned to a career of ignominy, sorting through the ledgers of dead companies to see which could be discarded whole and which needed to be shredded first. Reading number after number representing wealth he would never possess.

It happened one day that the man found a record of a great sum spent to build the concrete bones of a tower fifty stories tall—which was subsequently abandoned in the midst of the last financial crisis. That crisis had proved to be a wound in the side of the company until it staggered to the very death the banker was sorting through. No doubt distracted by its own death, the company had never found a buyer for the unfinished building.

It seemed a shame to the banker, as he returned to his work, that no one had ever purchased it. After all, he reasoned, it could have been demolished and the rubble resold. For a company, perhaps, such a project might not have seemed worth the trouble, but if a single man had held the title...

The banker began to rifle desperately through the papers in the box, but he could not find the title to that precious pile of concrete.

Nor could he the next day, or the next.

So he reported that all the files could be thrown away unshredded and he followed them to the landfill, where he would return each night to search for the slip of paper that could prove his greatest fortune.

38.

In a village that lay downriver from a chemical plant that belched colored smoke into the hazy sky, there was once an aging ewe who gave birth to a two-headed lamb.

All the other sheep in the flock were repulsed by the thing. They said it was bad enough to see such an ugly face once: it was unbearable to look away only to find another waiting for you. They hated the way it could watch them and watch them as they trotted by: they said it was an affront to nature, and had an evil eye. Sometimes they made crude comments about the mother, asking graphic questions about just how the thing had been sired.

But the mother sheep doted on it and called it her twoly beloved baby.

Among the other lambs born that spring there was one in particular who would pepper the hideous little lamb with insults, teasing her relentlessly about how her two faces would look better if they'd been crushed by stones, how her necks should be broken to keep her from looking into higher animals' eyes and to set her gazes where they belonged, on the slugs and the snails. And other spring lambs would baa and bleet in amusement, until a particularly obnoxious one of them snorted.

The disfigured, possibly-bewitched, and reputedly ill-conceived lamb hated that snorting.

Each night, after the tender two-headed monstrosity had spent a hard day being shunned, the mother bleated a lullaby to her little lamb until its four eyes fluttered closed and it fell to sleep. And the next day, when members of the flock pushed it away and refused to let it follow them—which is a grievous punishment for any sheep—the little lamb would sing the lullaby back to itself, improvising and modulating, its two heads singing now in unison, now in harmony.

The little lamb loved to sing and when it was left alone, almost out of sight of its woolly fellows (and out of earshot of derisive snorts and explicit references to the moment of its conception, as increasingly creatively popularly imagined), the lamb would fill the fields with renditions of its own melodies, rendered in majestic, if understandably sheepish, vibrato.

It happened once that the humans in the village celebrated a wedding, and sent a girl out to fetch a lamb to make curry. The girl, like the sheep, had always felt not only a little repulsed by the two-headed lamb, but also a little afraid of its unexpectedly soul-stripping gaze, and so she thought the time might be right to end the creature's life in a dish others would consume. But when she heard it singing so full and so sweetly, she turned—and chose the lamb that always taunted it instead.

The story's moral? Better to be a sweet lamb than to belong in a spiced curry.

39.

There was once a landfill where dwelt a cow named Bhuvanesh, several hundred mice, several thousand cockroaches, a smattering of stray dogs, and each night an accountant from the top four-fifths of his graduating class, who was off to seek his fortune.

The accountant whistled as he searched through discarded ledgers hour by hour for the lost title to a forgotten building in an abandoned part of town.

Each night, as he worked, anxiety gripped him. What if it rained and the title became waterlogged and molded over, lost beyond validity or even recognition? What if some rat had already found the thing and torn it to pieces to line her nest?

What if? What if? What if? he always said to himself, *you could waste away your life on what ifs.* Which would be a terrible fate for a man who had committed himself to the desperate pursuit of a longshot hypothetical.

And yet. No matter how many times the man told himself not to think about what ifs, with each passing night they loomed larger and time itself felt tighter and tighter until he could almost feel it begin to choke him, his breath growing rapid and shallow in the panic of that imminent asphyxiation.

Until, one night, under the light of a fickle moon—he found it.

40.

The prince.

The prince was locked in the tower.

Each day the prince pulled himself to his feet, a position that felt unnatural to one whose body was feigning death. Each day the prince pulled himself to his feet, and forced himself to walk across the tower, and the prince drank poison. Oh, he drank poison. He drank poison, he drank poison, thick and bitter and it burned his throat raw and rotted away the lining of his stomach.

The prince retched and retched and retched. The prince drank poison. He drank his poison.

And then he kept himself up and walked around the circumference of the narrow tower and he looked out its two small windows at the distant world of the living—oh he drank his poison, he drank his poison like a prince locked high in a tower thick and bitter and he retched.

The prince walked. The prince walked the tight circumference of the narrow tower again and again and then he let himself lie down because it felt right for one whose body feigned death.

41.

Once there was a girl who could sense shadows. Even from a great distance away she could feel them stretching as afternoon turned to evening, feel them tugging against their restraints as evening turned to night. She could feel them swirling through the city after nightfall, many of them wandering free as they slipped between the sporadic lights of the sleeping city. And sometimes, as it grew late, she could sense the shadows even shadows cast in places no eyes can see.

In the darkest parts of the city, far away from the highway sides where men burn trash to keep warm when the cold creeps in, she could feel those shadows gathering. In the darkest field, they would gather to dance and twirl, spinning around its dark heart, then bowing before their master.

The beast.

She had shaken the first time she sensed it, and she'd sensed it in every moment, waking or sleeping, ever since. The beast had hungry black pits for eyes. The beast had claws sharp enough to cut shadow. The beast could breathe in the slightest particle of light and exhale emptiness. Even across the city, the cold of it would sting against the back of her neck.

At first, the beast let the shadows gather to it, dance before it, offer pieces of the night to it.

But then the beast sensed her.

And the beast began to stalk her, circling slowly. Carefully. Sure as night, sharper than shadow, and starving.

Closing in.

42.

What am I? the frog cried from the bottom of the well one night, when a shadow fell across the moon and panic filled his throat. *Oh help me…what am I what am I what am I?*

43.

It was a fickle moon's night when the man with eight fingers finally found the one he was looking for. No mob boss or cutthroat. Not even one of those hot-blooded operatives for a cable company who cut down their rivals' cords. No, the man was, by the look of him, a second-rate bookkeeper. A soft-palmed accountant.

Could it be true that this man had the power to destroy a hidden civilization with eleven stories of homes, three stories of markets, two floors of shrines, and a governing brothel at the top? It seemed wrong to the old veteran, whose fingers had frozen against the metal of a rifle as he stood his country's ground at high elevation, that a piece of paper in a landfill could destroy so much. And yet: his vision showed him that it was so.

He strode across the field, over the garbage that was a testament to the appetites of this great metropolis, to confront the man. As he drew close, the accountant looked up and their eyes met. And just for a moment, the old veteran saw something in those eyes. Not malice. Not shrewd calculation. Not the dark pleasure of destruction. Just…hope.

"That paper means something to you?" the veteran asked.

The accountant shook. "Yes," he admitted. "It should not have been thrown away, and I have been looking for it for a long time."

The veteran studied the accountant. He clutched the paper protectively, longingly, almost lovingly. His eyes seemed to plead to be permitted to keep it, though fate itself had allowed the veteran to catch him in time.

"I can see it means a great deal to you," the veteran said. "And so it pains me to challenge you to a duel to the death for its possession."

44.

There was rain once. Rain that fell onto the improvised roofs of shantytown houses, drained down the streets to gather in cesspools, and remembered its past lives as it seeped down into the ground, picking up poisons that had gathered there before it was sucked up slowly through a pump and sprayed back out over a field.

The water remembered being a cloud and watching the earth below, remembered seeing the earth closer and closer and uglier and uglier, then striking it with unexpected violence and almost instant regret again and again and again.

The water remembered being one with the sea. Being one with the sea. Rising, gathering, falling. Rising, falling, gathering, and being one with the sea.

The water left the filth and poison it had been polluted with on the grain growing in the field. It rose again to fall again to flow again to gather again until it became again one with the sea.

One with the distant sea.

45.

There was a girl. There was a girl who could sense shadows but the beast sensed her and the beast came closer. The beast circled and circled, slowly, steadily, deadly, and the beast came always ever slightly slowly closer.

The girl wished to die. The girl wished to die. She wished to die before the beast came but she didn't want to die she just didn't want to exist any more when the beast came.

I'm sorry I exist, she said to no one, *I'm sorry I'm sorry I'm sorry I exist.*

But no one was listening so no one forgave her and the beast kept coming, creeping, circling closer.

46.

In a landfill not far from the airport of a great metropolis, beneath the silver light cast across space and through the atmosphere from the scarred face of the fateful moon, an accountant clutched a slip of paper tightly, longingly, almost lovingly, as he faced a grizzled-looking eight-fingered veteran.

"A duel to the death?" the accountant asked. "You would fight me to the death over a discarded piece of paper I dug with my own hands out of a landfill?"

The veteran glanced at the paper in his hands and nodded slowly. "That paper holds a power that is dear to me."

The accountant laughed. "This paper? No, you must be mistaken. The only power this paper holds is the power to blow up an old building and treat its remains as a cement mine. It would take a truly desperate man to dream of such a thing."

But rather than calming the veteran, the accountant's words seemed to enrage him. "On what terms shall our duel be, then? Would you prefer to be shot to death by my rifle? Or to stake your life on a game of cards?"

The accountant had never handled a rifle, and he knew he was terrible at cards. He shook his head.

The veteran grunted. "Shall we wrestle and see which one can throw the other?" He looked around, as if searching in vain for something. "I like that contest best when held at a great height."

The accountant shook his head again, panic rising within him.

"What shall it be?" the veteran spat. "What battle of skill or wits would you offer me for terms?"

The accountant tried and failed to keep his voice from shaking. "I have few enough skills and almost no wits," he admitted. He looked around him, hoping against hope he could think of a way to leave the landfill victorious and alive. And then an idea came to him. "Let us compete on even terms," he said. "At the end of an hour's time, let whoever can offer the other the greatest gift, without leaving this place to fetch it, be the victor."

The veteran laughed. "I agree to your terms," he said. "Though such a match will not be even."

47.

A long time ago, past several faraway countries, there was a sea pocked with rocky islands like the moon's face is scarred with craters. And deep within a jagged peak rising up from the sea to form one of those islands was a cave and in that cave there were chains and in those chains there were prisoners.

It was blacker than pitch in that cave, and that blackness was all the prisoners had ever known, for the crime for which they were imprisoned was none other than the crime of existence.

They lived in the dark, knowing nothing but the dark, not even knowing they had eyes, for who knows how long.

One of them could sense shadows, but she did not know that's what she sensed, because never having seen light, she had never seen shadow. So she had no word for the darkness she felt when the shadows danced, no word for the shadows even shadows cast that no eyes see.

Once. Once upon the timeless time of the cave too deep in the bowels of the island to know day or night. Once, as the prisoner girl sensed the shadows' shadows, their master saw her.

The beast.

And for the next days, or months, or lifetimes, it circled around her closer, closer, and the panic within her grew and grew. But she could not move, could not run. Because she was chained firm in the darkness, and because it wouldn't have helped. Running from the center of a circle can only lead toward the edge. Toward the beast's path.

The beast circled closer and still closer. Close. She could feel the cold empty of its breath filling the cave, could hear the silence of its beatless heart as it passed right behind her.

The girl grew angry. The girl screamed.

A pillar of fire erupted behind her and the girl and her fellow prisoners saw for the first time with their eyes.

They saw the shape of the beast's black shadow.

48.

The veteran lifted his hand before his face, looked through the gap where his fingers had once been, and marched off into a distant corner of the landfill.

After the veteran left, the accountant dug desperately, madly, haphazardly through the garbage. He begged fate to let some overlooked treasure fall into his hands. On previous nights of searching through box after box of files, he had noticed some fine marbles and a rusted knife lying along the wayside. He had hoped they would be enough to outdo his opponent, but the veteran's confidence left him shaken.

The accountant found a pile of worthless thousand-rupee notes, voided by the government in its demonitization drive. He found a few old film posters, the curves on the actresses crumpled, the hair of the heroes smudged with dirt. When the time was almost up, he found a strongbox.

The veteran was approaching again as the accountant pried it open with the rusted knife.

It was empty.

"Are you prepared to forfeit your life?" the veteran asked.

The accountant didn't trust his voice to answer without cracking.

49.

Once upon a time there was a girl who was juggling once upon a time and another once upon a time and a nightmare and a once upon a time and the truth yes the truth many truths good truths terrible truths and she could feel the emptiness as the beast breathed emptiness as the beast was coming closer closer and she was scared and she almost stopped juggling she almost let the light go out she almost decided to disappear into emptiness before the beast could take her there.

But she said once upon a time. Once upon a time. And she juggled, she juggled and she sensed the beast out of the corner of her mind as it circled her.

50.

Once upon a time. Yes, once upon a time there was a veteran and there was an accountant and there was a landfill down the street.

And this is what the veteran showed and told the accountant in the landfill where they dueled with gifts to the death.

"I have learned in the markets of my adopted home that worth comes from the needs and wants of the purchaser," the veteran began, "and so I'll offer you the choice between four treasures, not knowing in advance if each is truly greater than the last." He reached down into a tattered plastic shopping bag he had, no doubt, picked up along his way and began to reveal the gifts he had to offer.

The first glinted sharp and clear in the fickle moonlight. It was a hook, which appeared to once have served as a prosthetic for some man three fingers less fortunate than the veteran. "This hook," the veteran said, "sees the deep truth of things. Tragically, it cannot speak, but should I tear your throat out with it at the conclusion of our duel, you would feel the truth of your own life and know everything you have been and could be."

The veteran laid the hook down and produced a second item: an unbroken bottle made of deep green glass. "This bottle," the veteran said, "was made by a woman who had the power to capture time. Contained within its glass is rest deeper and sweeter than you have ever known: should you wish, it will ease you into the still deeper sleep of death."

After he laid the green glass bottle down beside the silver-colored hook, the veteran produced a pair of knitting needles. "I must warn you," he said, "that these needles were discarded because their previous owner found them to be very dangerous. They gave her great prosperity, but they also destroyed her home." The veteran gave the accountant a long, hard look before he continued. "The needles have a power the girl did not understand, a power the glassblower wished to have, though she never grasped what she wished for. These needles," he continued, "have the power to unknit time. For time can never simply be turned back: the way its twists our fates together must be unwoven, the paths laid separate once again." He paused. "With these knitting needles, you could unknit our fates in the moment before your execution and make it so we never had reason to meet."

Last of all, the veteran produced a simple clay bowl. "This earthen bowl," he said, "was the last worldly possession of a saint. One drink from it allows the partaker to instantly be freed from the cycle of captivating desire and released onto a purer plane." He looked at the bowl longingly. "Should you be given this bowl, it will not matter whether you die or live, as you will be beyond the cares of this world."

"These are the gifts I offer," the veteran concluded as he laid the clay bowl beside the hook, the glass bottle, and the knitting needles. "Is it possible you have anything to compare with the least of them?"

"Perhaps," the accountant said. "I offer you your life. Isn't a life, even in defeat, greater than any of these deaths?"

The veteran laughed. "Worth comes from the wants and needs of the purchaser," he said, "and my life means little enough to me." But his eyes strayed to the paper still grasped in the accountant's hand, the paper judges looked upon as granting the power of ownership, the paper which held the key to preservation or destruction over an apparently abandoned concrete tower in a dusty, forgotten, decrepit quarter of Mumbai. "If you would be the victor," the veteran told the accountant, "I would be happy enough to forfeit my life to you. You could easily offer me something worth far more."

51.

There were shadows in the night. There were shadows even in the darkness of the night. And the beast was tasting them, tearing them, annihilating them, but the beast was never full the beast was never full the best was never full.

52.

On a night when the moon was fickle and the omens poor, Malka the Madam of the Brothel left the room on the forty-seventh floor where she held court on matters both great and, in the veteran's absence, small, and descended with a number of the ladies of her council down a flight of stairs to the upper level of an elaborate complex of shrines.

Starting from one and continuing one by one to the others, she lit incense at each of them and gave offerings of food and drink. Fire on each stick of incense, smoke ascending into the air. Food grown from the earth, drink made of water.

Offerings of the four elements against the ill favor of this night. Offerings for the success of their trusted veteran's mission, and if possible, for his life.

53.

High in the mountains, there grew a gnarled tree, and woven into its twisted branches there was a nest, and in that nest sat a bird with three eyes and a magical shadow. A shadow that would bless all it touched with the power to see. Or the power to transform. Or else the power to see things for what they could be if transformed.

But when it felt the beast circling someone, the bird fled. The wind grew stiff and strong beneath its wings and it flew way, far away from the world of men. Away and away and away…

54.

Standing in a landfill he'd visited with a frequency that bordered on fidelity, the accountant considered his position.

For weeks—or was it months? or was it a lifetime? or was it a cycle of lifetimes upon lifetimes again and again and again?—he'd obsessed over a strange, serendipitous single chance at good fortune. For weeks, or months, or lifetimes, he had longed to change the person he was by first inhabiting and then obtaining a dream, no matter how difficult the way through the darkness to seize hold of it.

"This duel is difficult to decide," the accountant said to the veteran at last. "When all seemed hopeless, you showed me with a glance that victory had been, from the beginning, in my hand! And yet," he continued, "if I give you this paper, I am not only giving you the title to a forgotten building that could, when demolished, prove to be the source of some elusive wealth." He ran his fingers over the title: protectively, longingly, almost lovingly. "For me this paper has been so much more. It would be almost impossible for me to give you this paper, in fact, because we are all bound up by desire, and this *is* my desire."

The veteran's shoulders slumped. "Then it will be desire that undoes us all in the end."

"Perhaps," the accountant continued, "Or perhaps not. For I *can* imagine giving you this paper—but only because of a gift you offered me freely."

The veteran looked at him, baffled. "What gift is that?"

"An answer," the accountant said. "To a devious puzzle. For me to win this duel had seemed impossible, and yet with a glance you showed me how to turn defeat into victory, impossibility to certainty. And what is my desire for this paper, that building, some future fortune, at its root? Was it wealth I truly wanted, or the improbable victory it seemed to represent? I can see now I only wanted what every human being wants: to be part of a good story." The accountant handed the paper to the veteran. "And so," he said, "with this gift, I also grant you your life. Meager as its value may be, together their value is more than enough to leave me the victor."

The veteran wept and bowed low before the accountant. "By your grace," he said, "I accept this defeat."

"And with the story of this victory," the accountant said, "I find myself in a debt beyond calculation." And the accountant walked away home beneath the scarred moon's fickle light, as enlightened by the encounter as if he'd drunk from a saint's own bowl.

55.

The beast still stalked the girl. So steady, so slow, it almost startled her how close it had come. She could feel it circling closer, tighter, closer, could sense every time it sliced a shadow in half to feast on the emptiness that remains when a shadow is drained down to nothing but the husk of darkness.

The girl wanted to run, but she didn't know where. With the beast sweeping around her in those great circles, any distance she could go would only bring her closer to its path. She wanted to stay still and hope it could not see her, but it was clear from its movements that she was at their center. There was no hope that it had missed her.

No hope. No hope.

She had nowhere to go, but she still decided to prepare at once for the journey. If only she knew what she would need! The question troubled her until, while walking through a landfill near her home in the early hours of one morning, she happened to pass a discarded clay bowl.

The girl stopped and picked it up. If she had a bowl to carry food and gather water, what more could she need or long for?

Only a place to run. A place that was neither right nor left nor forward nor back. Not east not west not north not south.

Her thoughts stopped when she reached the base of a nearby tower. At once, she began to climb its walls.

56.

There are shadows and there are shadows. Shadows thinner than film and shadows that ooze thick across the floor. Shadows lighter than air and shadows so heavy they bend the floor and the walls and even the light around them.

In the jungle near a repentant village, a tiger felt a distant shadow tugging at a tiny, dark part of his heart. Pulling it like a needle, stabbing sharp tiny terrifying pain drawn in its wake.

57.

There once was a girl who had nowhere to run and no way to hide and so took to the air, climbing up the slick walls of a tall tower to escape the dark beast she could sense circling her closer, tighter, but now below, farther with each reach and push below.

The girl climbed until her hands ached, climbed as they bled, climbed until she came to a small window, and then climbed through into a small room next to a small hall that led around the circumference of the narrow tower.

A prince lay there, sleeping as though dead. He had lost his hair. The skin on different parts of his body looked burned. She could see it peeling away along his neck, peeling away around his eyes.

She could sense a shadow's shadow inside him.

It was, remarkably, shrinking. Tiny tendrils of decay spread around it in the shapes a shadow's shadow might reach, but the things no longer reached for him, no longer feasted on him.

The prince had convinced it that he was dead.

As she looked at his body, slumped against the tower's cold floor, the gentle movement of his chest with each breath could barely convince *her* otherwise.

He was starving the shadow, to be sure, but what would his gambit be worth if in the process he killed himself?

She knelt beside the prince, then leaned over and touched him, ever so lightly, trying not to disturb the skin where it was peeling as if burned.

He startled awake, no doubt bewildered to find another human so high in this prison of a tower.

His eyes were wild as he looked up at her. "What are you?" he asked.

And the question echoed in her mind. *What am I what am I what am I?*

58.

There are shadows and there are shadows.

Shadows that are silent, shadows that sigh out the end of their existence, shadows that scream as they are torn to pieces.

There are also shadows that smile dark when they have been fed.

59.

There was rain. There was rain once and once and once and once that fell and fell and fell and fell from the sky to the earth and from the sky to earth and once it fell past a tower.

In the tower, there lived a prince who dragged himself to his feet to drink poison, thick and bitter, that burned his throat and rotted away the lining of his stomach. And beside him there walked a girl who could see the shadow within and told him it was dying and warned him that he might, too.

And the prince said, "So be it."

But the girl shook her head and said: no.

And she walked with him all around the circumference of the narrow tower. Walked again and again, though she felt the beast circling with them, almost beneath them now, so close it could have touched her shadow but still stories and stories below. The girl fought down her own panic, and she walked with the prince. Walked with him around and around, again and again until he collapsed.

And then she took a clay bowl in her hand and she reached out the window.

The rain gathered into the bowl. And the rain remembered so many things, but nothing like this bowl. The rainwater rested. The rainwater rested and was still and the girl brought the bowl back through the small window into the tower and the rain was at peace.

The girl looked at the prince, and her eyes told the prince she wanted him to live. Her eyes seemed to long for life so badly he forgot for a moment how crucial it was that he cling close to death.

And so the prince drank water from the clay bowl. And it was sweet to him, so sweet, though it stung his burned throat and settled uneasy in his stomach.

It doesn't matter, he thought, *if I die or if I live. At last I feel at peace.*

And as soon as he drank from the clay bowl, the girl saw the shadow fall away from him and sink, like a cesspool, onto the floor.

60.

The prince could feel something in him change as he looked at the girl who had scaled the walls of the tower and given him fresh water in a simple clay bowl. "What are you?" he asked her once again.

He had asked her before in a bewildered delirium. Now he asked, bowed low to the stone floor, in awe.

But the girl didn't answer. Her eyes were fixed onto a shadowy spot on the floor near him.

"What is it?" the prince asked. "What's wrong?"

And then he tried to scream, but the scream got trapped in his throat. Because he saw a beast with empty black eyes cutting through the shadow and pulling itself up through the floor.

1.

Once upon a time. Once upon a time a girl stood her ground in time and faced the beast as it emerged: first through the floor, then almost at the same time through the ceiling and the walls and it circled around her and it breathed in the light so that the tower was darker than night, dark as a cave buried deep in the bowels of the earth. And the beast breathed out emptiness against the back of her neck, so strong that it made her shiver. Emptiness against her throat, and she started to shake.

She was tired. She was terrified. She felt exhausted, empty, wishing only that she had died before the beast fixed its empty black eyes on her and it came close so close.

Then she grew angry.

Who was the beast to circle her?

Who was the beast to fill her thoughts and haunt her dreams and weigh down even her stories?

Who was the beast? Who was the beast?

What are you? the girl thought. *What are you?*

She forced a scream out past where it wanted to lodge in her throat, let out at last a scream that had been waiting inside her long long she didn't know how long. And a pillar of fire erupted behind the beast, a pillar of fire that lit up the face of the prince, that let her see him so clearly she could catch her own reflection in his eyes.

She screamed, and the fire surged toward the beast. The beast howled a soundless howl and it staggered.

But it did not die.

Then the girl wept. And with the torrent of her tears, the rain burst through the window with terrible violence and the rain struck the beast without mercy or regret: lashed him drop after drop ten thousand and one drops, and the beast staggered back and back.

But still, the beast did not die.

So the girl took a deep breath and the wind rushed to her, rushed in through the tower's two small windows. It rushed around the beast, circling, circling, faster and faster, until it formed a whirlwind that tore at the beast.

And the beast staggered. The beast stumbled. The beast fell.

But still, the beast did not die. Though struck by fire, water, wind—the beast did not die.

So the girl took the clay bowl she had found in the landfill and she crushed it in her hands to dust and she sprinkled the broken earth over the beast.

And the beast collapsed in on itself, swallowed by its own emptiness.

The prince looked at her in the dying light of embers of fire still lying scattered on the tower's stone floor. "What are you?" he asked.

"Me?" the girl said. "I am Razia Shah."

And all across the world, magic mirrors broke and prisoners were set free. The rain remembered it was one with the sea and a frog drank deeply of sweet waters in a well. A tiger's heart was freed and a magical bird returned to its mountain nest.

And for the first time in a long time, a juggler stopped juggling and rested.

This happened. All of it happened.

Once upon a time.

AMIR MOUSA AND THE LIBERATION OF BIR QALAM

THE WEEK after he celebrated his seventieth birthday, Amir Mousa worked nearly seventy hours at his EZ Way Grocery store selling cigarettes, cheap porn, Doritos, HoHos, potato chips, beer, cokes, and other worthless shit to trapped people who were going nowhere in their lives. People who reminded him that he was going nowhere, either, that he would probably never escape the trash heap that passed for a neighborhood on this side of the I-85 underpass outside downtown Greensboro, that he hadn't been truly happy in sixty-three years and four months. That he hadn't felt whole since the day the Israeli Defense Forces had forcibly evacuated Bir Qalam—a week before Christmas, no less!—and then razed it before its inhabitants came back, putting an end to the old Mousa family business and to the village that for a countless generations had been their home.

Yes. Amir had lost home, and then gradually also hope, so that now at seventy he thought rest was a moment like this when all the customers were busy browsing or glued to a video gambling machine so you could watch the TV for a minute before someone else walked in.

This time it was a fat girl with long sweat streaks down her shirt. She walked up to the register like she owned the place but was looking to sell.

"I want a orange juice please," she said.

"Juice is over there," said Amir pointing. "You get a bottle, you bring it here."

"I'm thirsty!" she said. Like asking her to get her own damn juice was a death sentence.

"This place is self-serve," said Amir. And then he turned back to the TV so she'd know he didn't care about her or her thirst. She didn't move. The anchor was talking about the unemployment rate, a graph was showing what a mess the country might be in again soon, and running across the bottom of the screen was the winning number from the Mega Millions drawing the night before. Luckily Amir hadn't checked his ticket yet, so that at least gave him something to do. He pulled it out from under the counter and made a show of squinting at the TV screen.

The first five numbers matched. Suckers' hope started to swell in Amir's chest.

"Where is it then?" said the girl. Why was she still standing there?

"Don't talk now," said Amir. He tried to keep track of the numbers on his ticket and on the scrolling banner at once. Same number on the screen and his card. Same number. Same.

"Where's the juice at?" the girl said again.

Then the mega-ball. *Same number.*

"No juice!" said Amir. His eyes ran over the ticket, checking again. And again. He must've missed something. He wasn't a man who won things. And yet—now, somehow, against the longest possible odds, he had.

After so many years, he'd beat this country. He had won. He looked out over the shop he'd run for years and smiled. "Everyone!" he announced. "We are closed *right now.* Get out of the store."

"But I'm thirsty," said the girl. "And I've been wait—"

"Shut up," said Amir and he laughed in her fat face. "I'm sure you can find some water at your home."

The week after his seventieth birthday, Amir Mousa finally got to throw out his customers, roll down the steel security grille over the EZ Grocery storefront for good, and walk away from it all.

As soon as he got into his car, he took out his cell phone and called his cousin Elias to tell him about the jackpot.

"It's fate," Elias said. "Fate smiling on our family again at last. How much money?"

"Four-hundred million."

Elias whistled and then fell silent. That's why Amir had called him first—he knew he wouldn't jabber about it like a horny bird or scream his head off like some American idiot who knows she's on TV. You could trust Elias to treat a miracle with reverence.

"You be careful," Elias said. "Those lottery people—can you really trust them?"

"I'm not going to sign a thing until I can get your Yacoub to help me. I'm not going to let some corrupt sons-of-bitches take it all from me now."

Even over the phone, Amir could hear his cousin let out a deep breath. "What are you going to do with the money?" Elias asked.

"You know me, *ibn al-Am*. All I ever wanted is to get Bir Qalam back."

Fourteen people had come to Amir's birthday party. Fifty-eight came to the first family planning session after he hit the jackpot, driving down in vanloads or arriving on planes from London or Dubai or Singapore to represent branches of the family there. Amir had to send a niece down to Dollar Tree to buy out their supply of plastic lawn chairs so all the adults could have a place to sit. And then he had to send a nephew on another run to buy extra tables to hold all the food people brought to share for dinner.

Amir watched Yacoub work his way through the crowd. When he'd been on the phone all day with the lottery people and his stockbroker friends and international lawyers and Greek real estate agents, he'd kept his suit jacket on no matter how hot and humid it got in Amir's house. He still wore his work shirt, now, but with the sleeves rolled halfway up and the top button undone. Called out greetings to cousins looking for parking halfway down the block as they got in, who leaned out their windows and shouted, "Hey Jimmy!" back. Jimmy. Like they were afraid to use his real name. Or maybe had forgotten it had also been the name of Amir's paternal uncle.

When everyone had finished greeting and eating, Yacoub stood up told the joke about the man back in Palestine who brought two bags of sand across a checkpoint each day. The man kept getting pulled off his bike and detained by a group of IDF soldiers, who rifled through his sand-filled bags and strip searched him, convinced he was up to no good. No matter how they tried, though, they couldn't work out just what his crime was. Civilians pressured to inform finally shared rumors that he was a smuggler, but no search could identify anything of value in the bags. "They never did realize," Yacoub said, "that all he'd been smuggling was bicycles."

And then Yacoub reminded them about Amir's money and describing how he was going to take care of it vividly and step-by-step, just like it was another good story. He explained how he weaved his ways through lottery policies like it was a maze to escape. He'd talk about tax laws like they were the forces of evil and about loopholes he'd found like they were saintly Orthodox priests who drove the darkness away. He talked about investments like new friends and projected growth like old wine. And everyone would laugh and clap every time he'd mention a big number.

When Yacoub had them all practically drunk with stories of Amir's wealth, he turned suddenly serious. "We didn't invite you here, though, just to tell you about one success in our family. We asked you to come so you could hear uncle's dream—which we hope you'll want to be a part of. I can't tell you his dream like he can. I carry it in my bones, but he saw it with his own eyes. So I want you to pay close attention to what he has to tell you tonight."

Amir looked out from his chair over the faces of the people who filled his lawn. That boy had Amir's father's chin; this girl had his mother's eyes. He could have wept for how much he missed both of them this night. "Sometimes people ask me what I think of this country," Amir said. "And I tell them I wouldn't trade the whole America for *one inch* of our Palestine." He let the words hang for a moment in the muggy warmth of this place. If the children remembered one thing in their lives, he wanted them to remember that.

He could see the fireflies coming out in the little wooded area at the back of the yard. "Between the folks at Mega Millions and Yacoub, there's a lot of people telling me lately I'm a very rich man," he said. "But what does that get you here? You get a nice, quiet place—they just build a freeway next to it in ten years. You think you have a nice neighbor? He's gonna get a new job or maybe lose his old one and then he's gonna move away. Why? What for?"

Amir looked at Elias. "When we were boys, a person five blocks away knows everything about you—knows your family, knows your name. If you get sick, five people are there that same day with soup, with bread, with an hour to sit by you." He looked at the little kids again. "Hundreds of years before Tide, our family was making soap out of pure olive oil. You use the same soap to wash your body and your hair and you never get dandruff. That's what life was like in Bir Qalam."

For a moment, he let himself be a six-year-old again, playing next to the village boys on the beach by the Mediterranean. Then he raised his voice. "With the money, we're going to buy the soil of Bir Qalam back from under the feet of the Israelis and we're going to get it out of there to rebuild our village somewhere no Zionist terrorist is ever gonna reach." Amir blinked back tears of old anger and fresh relief. "And I want you all to come live with me there."

Yacoub called three weeks later from Athens to tell Amir he'd found a perfect island in the Aegean for twenty million Euros. "It's pretty close, which will save on shipping costs for the soil, and it's definitely a buyers' market in Greece," he said. "Do you want to come take a look at it?"

Amir trusted Yacoub's judgment on details like this. "Not until you've brought the soil where our house was," he said.

Yacoub laughed, but it sounded shallow and forced. "I'll tell them you'll take the island, then," he said. "But uncle, you really should come set up here now. It's got a beautiful beach, clean air—you're retired now, you've earned it."

Didn't Yacoub understand? "I don't care about a Greek beach," Amir said. "I want my home."

Yacoub seemed agitated. "Uncle, it's not so easy. We still haven't got all the landholders signed on to sell. And even when we do—the Israelis aren't stingy with red tape."

"If they want a bribe, we can give a small bribe, but I'm not coming out to some island when it's nothing but an island," Amir said.

Yacoub sighed. "I just want you to be happy, uncle."

But Amir refused to be hurried. "I've waited almost sixty-four years. I can wait a few more months."

Yacoub didn't answer for a minute and Amir wondered if they'd lost the signal. It was nothing but pain doing business on the Mediterranean from here. "Hello? Hello, Yacoub?" Amir said.

"I'm still here," said Yacoub. "I'll get the paperwork for the island ready and fax it over to Hala. She'll bring it you—sign it right away and let her send it back. Don't try to mail it yourself this time, hey?"

"I won't," said Amir. "You don't worry about it. Thank you."

"I'll fly back to Tel Aviv tonight and drive up to the village tomorrow. I'll get this done as fast as I can for you, uncle."

And then Yacoub was off again into his rush-rush M.B.A. rhythm of life. Amir wondered what he'd be like when he got the chance to really settle down.

Just a few hours later, Yacoub's wife Hala pulled up in her scratchless black BMW and let Leila and Maria out of the backseat while she unbuckled Imil. Amir poured glasses of juice and filled a bowl with cashews for the two little girls and then got some dates and started coffee for Hala. She would probably tell him she didn't want coffee, that she wasn't going to stay long and could just have a glass of juice like the girls, but once she caught the scent of it, he suspected she'd stay long enough for the slow-brewed Turkish coffee anyway.

"I've got the papers Jimmy sent for you," Hala said once she'd laid out a blanket and let down Imil on it. "He said the place is a dream. It's crazy, isn't it? Our very own island?"

Amir flipped through the packet Hala gave him looking for the spots that needed his signature. "I don't understand how Yacoub can keep track of all this. I can't even follow a paragraph, and in his mind he can understand pages and pages." He looked over at Hala. She was enjoying the dates: good. "Your husband—I think he's some kind of genius."

"He's very good at what he does," she said. "Just like *ammu* was, I've heard."

"My dad was amazing, but he never had to deal with all these papers and papers. Trust was the contract in those days. So it was faces he remembered: traders from the Gulf and Egypt and Turkey he knew he could trust."

"And you guys did pretty well?"

"The best. Everyone in town trusted my father," he said. "That's better than any bank account." Amir glanced at the children's faces and smiled. "You're going to love raising your kids in the village," he told her. "I wish I'd been able to raise mine there."

Hala shrugged. "We've done all right growing up here, too."

Did she really think that? Amir couldn't tell if she was being polite, trying to appease the guilt of his generation for raising a homeless people, or if she was genuinely satisfied with the rootless way she'd grown up. Could an olive tree branch, abandoned on strange soil, somehow turn itself in to an unruly vine? The thought left him feeling unsettled.

"Let me go check on the coffee," Amir said.

He came back with the cup and set in front of Hala. She let it sit there, probably waiting for it to cool off. "Do you trust Jimmy?" she said. "The way your dad trusted his business partners, I mean."

"Of course I trust your husband," Amir said. "He's my nephew and he's a smart man. I'd trust him with anything."

Hala smiled wistfully. "I really don't understand where he came from," she said. "The world doesn't make men like him anymore." She took a careful first sip of her coffee. "I hope you understand what he's up against."

Amir nodded slowly. He might not follow the financial and legal details, but he understood all too well what Yacoub was up against. Amir had felt the weight of the world. It had almost crushed him.

Amir was more careful afterwards to give Yacoub all the encouragement he could and made sure to sign any paper Hala brought him right away. Yacoub responded by working harder than ever. He kept calling to give updates whenever he could, and had Hala call and read from his emails when things got too busy. There were fewer little decisions, though, which Amir had to worry about.

Which gave him time to focus on tracking down old friends from the village instead. He found one of the boys he used to play *al-manyya* with in Australia, then another in Bahrain and a third in Honduras. He found the younger brother of a girl he used to admire now living in Jordan and then found her family in Toronto. And he told all of them about his plan to bring the village back and promised to call again when it was ready.

In August, Yacoub called to say he had good news and bad news. The bad news was that their attempt to push everyone into a sale by tying together the transactions into a single contract had failed—some of the local landholders were just too stubborn. The good news was that most of the old village area now belonged to absentee landlords in Tel Aviv and Los Angeles who were happy to sell the land out from under their tenants for what the Mousa Corporation was willing to offer.

"Mousa Corporation?" said Amir. "Our surname is a company now?"

"There's more than that, Uncle," Yacoub said. "Actually I've set up several different companies. I know it's a lot to keep track of—be sure to let me know if you have questions about any of the paperwork. Mousa Incorporated operates here; Bir Qalam International handles business in Europe and will carry most of the construction accounts; Ammu Amir LLC is over investments in the United States, and Imil Ocean Incorporated shields some of your assets from tax." Yacoub laughed. "You like the names I picked for our little corporate family?"

Amir appreciated Yacoub's work, but he couldn't help but feel that his nephew was avoiding something. "When will the land from my father's house arrive on the island?" he asked.

"That's very difficult, uncle," said Yacoub.

"Difficult?" said Amir. "Difficult how?"

"That land belongs to one of the holdouts. It may take a long time."

Amir tried to keep his voice under control. "You mean the *title* belongs to him. The land belongs to our family."

"Uncle, Lev Fridman is a very stubborn man."

"Lev Fridman?" A Russian Jew. Amir had nothing against Jews, only against Zionists. But the immigrant Russians were all Zionists—not one of them belonged there. One of the *Mizrahim*, the Middle Eastern Jews, Amir could have talked with, but for a Russian to refuse to sell him his own home—it was unbearable.

Yacoub interrupted Amir's anguish. "Can I tell you some more good news?"

Amir said nothing. He didn't know what to say.

"It took more money than I wanted, but we found a friend in the development ministry who helped us accelerate the timetable on the environmental impact study. We can start shipping the land in just a few days now." Amir should have been excited, but he still felt numb. "Fridman will sell eventually—we'll make sure of it," Yacoub said. "But please don't wait until then to come out to the island. We can have a house ready for you soon enough."

"No," said Amir. "You can start bringing in members of the family, and I'll give Hala a list of Bir Qalam people to fly in. But I wait until my father's land is ready for me."

Amir was sorting through old photographs to send the architects when Yacoub called a few days later.

"That list you sent," Yacoub said, "it's pretty long, and a lot of those people have an awful lot of grandchildren. Do we really have to invite them all to come?"

"It's their right to return to the land they belong to," said Amir. "It would be a crime to take that right away." He was surprised Yacoub of all people had asked.

"I'm sorry," said Yacoub. "I know that. It's just—look, it's not just land and airfare subsidies. We'll have to import extra olive trees. The groundwater is deep on the island, and we're going to need bigger wells than I'd budgeted for. And more people means more work to protect the new soil from erosion. This all costs money. And if we're not prepared to spend it, do you want to watch your new village wash away?"

Amir's head hurt. "I'm seventy years old. We can spend all the money if we need to—I'm not trying to save anything for a rainy day after this is taken care of."

But Yacoub was still agitated and he spent a long time talking about how the money was set up in an annuity rather than a lump sum, and how he could have Hala bring Amir some graphs showing the initial outlays and their monthly financial commitments compared with dividends their companies made.

"I don't want to look at graphs," said Amir. "Can you just tell me in plain English what is the problem and what can we do about it?"

"Maybe it would help to bring in some other partners," said Yacoub. "I've met some investors in the Gulf who might be interested in sharing the risks on this project with us."

Amir hesitated. He didn't want to work with anyone outside the village if he didn't have to, but what if the only other choice was turning people away? "If that's what it takes, and if you trust these men, go ahead," said Amir. "But we don't leave one inch of land and we don't turn away one single person who came from Bir Qalam."

"I'll see what I can do, uncle."

"Not an inch," said Amir. "If we have to, we tear the land out during the night from Lev Fridman."

"We'll find a way to get the land from Fridman," said Yacoub, his voice growing tense again. "I wish you wouldn't worry about that so much."

Amir got the first letter from Bir Qalam that November from Elias, who sent pictures of side of the island they'd built up so far, of the olive trees, and of an old-style oil press they'd bought out of Gaza.

On Christmas, Hala showed Amir a picture she'd been emailed by Amal's grandson Daud, who was a Greek Orthodox priest, of the tiny church he was building in Bir Qalam. A week later, she brought a picture of the crowd of at least a hundred and fifty that gathered all around the church ground and onto the narrow village street for the first Christmas mass there. Amir called Yacoub and asked if he'd made any progress with Lev Fridman—Yacoub said he hadn't, but promised to meet with Fridman in person again if he could.

He did in early January, and Fridman still wouldn't sell for any price. Said his father was a Zionist who died in a Russian gulag, and he wouldn't trade one inch of Israel for all the money in the world. Amir hated him passionately for that. "No one loves gold so much as a thief," he said to Jimmy. "But what right does he have?"

On the first day of February, three inches of snow fell on Greensboro overnight. Elias happened to call that night and laughed, then told Amir it was sixty degrees in Bir Qalam.

"Forget the Russian," Elias said. "It's beautiful here. You should come."

"No," Amir said. He couldn't go back on his words now.

"If you won't come to live, then at least come as my guest," said Elias.

"There's nothing I want more than to embrace you on the streets of our village again," said Amir. "But until my father's land is there, you know I can't come."

In March, a month before Amir Mousa's seventy-first birthday, Lev Fridman was the only Israeli left with any title to land in what had been Bir Qalam. Amir couldn't sleep well, and started losing his appetite, and not even the letter from Hala with a picture of her girls with their grandfather could console him. Not even the news from Yacoub that over six hundred Palestinian Christians and six wealthy investors from Bahrain now owned homes on his island could give him rest.

They held a giant birthday party with a goat-meat barbecue and all-night dance for Amir in Bir Qalam, but he refused to come. Daud's brother Salim flew all the way out to Greensboro with a cake made in Bir Qalam for him and helped Amir watch the party by Skype.

It was too bad Salim had to miss the party, because it looked like a lot of fun. Amir wasn't very good company to compensate: it took most of his energy just to eat enough birthday cake to keep the guests from worrying about him. He got tired of watching the party on Skype pretty early, but stayed up until it was eight p.m. in North Carolina and three a.m. on the island so his failing interest wouldn't spoil the fun.

At midnight, Amir's phone rang. It was Yacoub, calling from Tel Aviv.

"Happy birthday, uncle," Yacoub said.

"It was a great party," said Amir. "You should have stayed and danced with your wife—it's not good for you to always work so much."

"How could I stay?" said Yacoub. "I couldn't stand to, when I should be looking for a way to get you to the village your money built."

Amir felt despair like a stone in his gut. "It's not your fault," he said. And he thought about the depth of his hate for Lev Fridman, who tore families apart and ruined old men's birthdays and would probably laugh if he knew he had kept an olive-skinned Palestinian man from dancing with his wife and listening to the singing of his children.

"I've been thinking about it, uncle," said Yacoub. "Fridman isn't going to sell, and we can't let you sit around and hope that he's the first of you two to die."

"I'm not moving without that land," said Amir. "And if you're thinking we should murder the Russian, it's a bad idea no matter how you're planning to hide it."

Yacoub laughed long and loud. "I don't want to kill Lev Fridman, uncle, but I think I might have an idea."

"What? What is it?" Amir felt hopeful again for the first time in weeks. If Yacoub really had a plan, maybe he'd celebrate with a midnight snack.

"It would be risky," said Yacoub, "and extremely expensive. You'd have to decide how much you're willing to stake on the plan, but I think it will work."

Anything. Anything for that land. Anything to beat the Zionist Russian. "I'll do it," said Amir. "No matter how much is the risk."

"All right," said Yacoub. "Then we try to take it through forced erosion."

"What?" said Amir.

"You told me once you want that land if we had to yank it out from under him. Well, the engineers for the new Bir Qalam taught me that's just what will happen if you leave soil next to the sea unprotected." Yacoub took a deep breath. "So really, all we need to do is bring the sea forward a few acres. If Fridman gets scared and sells, we get the land that way. If Fridman doesn't sell, we gather the soil in tight mesh nets as it washes away until his house collapses."

"You can catch the soil? You're sure?"

"It'll be difficult to move the sea and then catch the land, yes—that why it's so expensive. But I talked to Mousa Corporation's chief engineers, and they say we could do it. Fridman may try to get a court injunction against us, but we should be able to fight it off for long enough to finish the job if we hurry. He'll probably sue us afterward, too, but even if they give him the ten times the market worth of the property in a settlement it'll be less than we've already offered him."

"Do it!" said Amir. He got up and made his way down the hall toward the kitchen and the fridge. He felt the best he had in months.

This was about even more than his home now. About more than the land his father and his father before him and his father before him for generations had lived on.

Amir Mousa was going to teach one stubborn Zionist what it was like to have your home snatched out from under you, and it was going to be the most satisfying thing he'd done in his life.

The week after Amir's seventy-first birthday, bulldozers stated digging deeper into the ground around his ancestral home. Lev Fridman probably just thought they wanted more Palestinian soil—Yacoub said he didn't do a thing to stop them.

When the bulldozers had gotten close enough to the Mediterranean that water started seeping in, Yacoub said Fridman ran out of his house and started screaming at the drivers. He thought they were making a mistake. They'd been smart enough to play along and called Yacoub saying they'd clear up the problem. And then as soon as Fridman fell asleep that night they breached to remaining bar enough to keep the water flowing in nice and strong.

Hala flew into Greensboro the next day with the kids and took Amir out to Talulla's to celebrate.

Yacoub called Amir every day after that to keep him updated. First Yacoub reported that he'd gone to Fridman, pretended to apologize, and offered to buy the damaged property for ten percent more than his last offer. But Fridman had just called him a lying son of a whore and thrown him out of the house. Soon Fridman had called the police and tried to have the construction workers arrested, but luckily Yacoub had taken the precaution of forging some permits to buy the workers a little more time.

When the work didn't stop and the water kept getting closer, Fridman sought an injunction on the construction from the local court, but the judge was waiting to rule until his clerks could find the original copies of the permits that had been issued. Fridman left a long, angry message accusing Yacoub of trying the steal Israeli land, but Yacoub told Amir that if it got out, Fridman would just sound paranoid.

Yacoub left a message with Fridman and even sent him a letter to tell him they were still working on closing the accidental breach to the sea, but that his engineers had suggested there may be safety issues if Fridman stayed in the house. He included an offer to pay for property damage or to buy up the property outright.

"The better the paper trail that we tried to help him, the harder it will be for him to get much in court," Yacoub said to Amir. The boy was sharp. There was no denying that—Elias's son was a genius.

Amir waited for the phone call each day to tell him how justice was creeping closer.

In May, Lev Fridman's house collapsed. Fridman had been in it at the time and the construction workers rushed over to pull him out of the rubble, then drove him to the hospital to take care of his broken leg. While he was in the hospital, they quickly harvested the rest of the soil, closed the breach, and started pumping the water back out to the sea again. Yacoub offered to pay medical expenses and property damage and to buy the title to the property if Lev wanted to sell.

Lev kept the title to the land, but Amir was willing to settle for the top six feet.

Amir knelt down and kissed the ground when the boat brought him at last into Bir Qalam. It was so good to be home after so very long. They threw him another party, where he danced until four a.m. and drank too much. After he'd spent three days mostly sleeping off the alcohol and the jet lag, he and Elias took the kids out and taught them how to play *al-manyya*. Leila and Maria looked so healthy in the Mediterranean sun, and their laughter carried across the island like bird songs.

"You're pretty sweaty, old man," said Elias as they sat and caught their breath. And he gave Amir a bar of pure olive oil soap. Just holding it and smelling it brought so many memories back. And holding soap again, made in his village, seems to wash the memories clean of all the pain with which they'd been tainted for so very, very long.

Yacoub had an office up in one of the Bahraini investor's mansions over on the other side of the island, but he always walked back down to Bir Qalam for a cup of coffee in the afternoon. One day he brought a letter from the Israeli government to show: a judge had issued an injunction order on their unauthorized construction until further notice.

"Can you believe it?" Yacoub said. "We're like the bicycle smuggler. The trick is only clever because the Israelis are such stupid bureaucrats!"

They laughed long and hard over that letter. Oh, how they laughed.

Yacoub wasn't laughing a month later when the Israelis issued a warrant for his arrest on charges of forgery, export duty evasion, criminal neglect, and attempted homicide on Lev Fridman.

"How can they say I tried to kill him?" Yacoub asked Amir. "I sent him a letter of warning!"

Elias thought Yacoub should fly straight back to Tel Aviv and fight the charges, and Hala suggested he counter-sue Fridman for slander. But Amir warned him to be careful, because a Palestinian could never know what to expect from Israeli justice. Especially if they realized that Yacoub was living in a Palestinian village that had been depopulated in 1948 but recently and permanently liberated from Israeli occupation.

So Yacoub put his Israeli lawyer to work fighting on the case and then sailed back to Athens and took several Greek MPs out to nice dinners in case he had to fight extradition further down the road.

A few weeks later Amir went up to one of the Bahraini's mansions at Yacoub's invitation to watch a rebroadcast on Hiraklion's Kriti TV of a Tel Aviv Channel 10 special about the Lev Fridman case. The special showed footage of the old site of Bir Qalam, which had since flooded again so that it looked like a tiny, shallow bay. Lev Fridman shouted accusations at the camera about what had happened, said all sorts of bad things about Yacoub and the Mousa Corporation. But who would believe him?

Then the special got worse. It blew the faked permits issue out of proportion, ignored the letters and suggested Yacoub had meant for Fridman to die, told about Amir's lottery win and interviewed old customers who said he'd get angry if you so much as said the word Israel in front of him and that he hated America.

The special suggested he was funding terrorists with money from the jackpot.

An American Congressman promised to investigate.

Yacoub turned the TV off and turned to Amir. "I don't know how to play this, uncle," Yacoub said. "That money is very important for us."

"We have the village now," said Amir. "What can they do to us?"

"It's more difficult than that," said Yacoub. "A lot of things we already paid for, but on all the land, even on this island, we're still making payments out of the annuity. If I try to switch to a lump sum and get all the money out now, it looks bad. But if I leave it in and they decide to freeze your assets, we're in trouble."

"I lived forty-six years in America," Amir said. "I've got rights."

"They don't take it lightly if they think you're funding terrorism," said Yacoub. "And we've spent enough on plane tickets for Palestinians this year it's bound to set off a red flag somewhere."

"Pull it out fast then," Amir said. He didn't care how he looked to America so long as they didn't have any power over him. He'd thought maybe he'd visit one more time to see the woods in Greensboro or eat at Talulla's again, but he could give that all up and count it as a fair sacrifice for what he had.

It turned out a Bir Qalam resident named Zahi actually did have some ties to groups the Americans counted as terrorist organizations, so it went all over the news when it came out that Amir's companies had paid for his flight and flights for many other Palestinians, and there were accusations that even more of Amir's money had gone through Zahi to embargoed organizations. Lucky that Yacoub had traded in the annuity for a lump sum, paid off the rest of the island loans, and gotten a few extra hundred-thousands transferred to Imil Ocean Inc. in the Bahamas right away, because all their American assets, from Amir Ammu LLC to the hundred and seventy dollars left in Amir's Wells Fargo Account, were soon frozen.

"How can they call us 'terrorists'?" said Amir. "Menachem Begin, he was a real terrorist. Did they freeze the accounts of

Jews who gave to him? That Lev Fridman—he's a terrorist. Saying Yacoub tried to murder him when he lived on the land murderers stole from my father."

But the Israelis kept listening more and more to Lev Fridman. Yacoub's lawyer released the letters, but Israelis thought the high offering price on the land was evidence that Yacoub had been plotting something—because Israelis didn't know what it was like to be the last one born on land you've had for countless generations. Israeli diplomats made threatening statements toward Greece about Yacoub, and soon Yacoub was having to spend all night in talks with members of the Greek government.

If Yacoub were not so completely likeable, if he had not been so careful from the beginning to cultivate sympathy and trust in key corners of the political establishment, the Greek government might have given in. But somehow Yacoub managed to make it a point of pride for them, an assertion of their own sovereignty in the face of a hostile international order, to protect him.

When Fridman saw he couldn't get Yacoub extradited, he sued Mousa Incorporated in civil court. The trial made big news in Israeli papers, and Amir had to laugh when he saw the Israels start to recognize what he'd done to them. He was still laughing when the jury awarded Fridman a record-setting settlement.

"We'll have nothing left when it's done," said Yacoub. "And I don't know how long the Greeks will protect me if we don't pay."

"Just pay him," said Amir. "We have Bir Qalam, and that's enough."

Yacoub sighed. "We have the village, but we need money to keep the villagers. They respect you, uncle, but without the money I don't know if they're strong enough in your vision. I understand the value of the kind of life you're trying to give us, but they're used to something else."

Amir didn't see what money had to do with them. The flight had already been paid for, as had the homes made to match ones that had been razed in the disaster. "What are you saying?" Amir asked.

Yacoub took a deep breath and Amir watched him let the tension in his body go. "You gave me your dream, and you gave me the power to make it real," Yacoub said. He gave Amri a small, courageous smile. "I shouldn't worry now. We'll use your money to pay the settlement, and I swear to you I will find a way to care for the village you gave us."

"I trust you," said Amir. "Whatever problem is troubling you, I believe you can solve it."

Things quieted down in the village after they paid on the settlement. Since all Amir's companies were completely bankrupt, from Mousa Corporation to Imil Ocean Inc., Yacoub got a job with his Bahraini partners. They let him manage different projects in Turkey and the Gulf, and he even talked them into launching some kind of computer business for Daud's brother Salim—Amir never saw Salim build or sell a single computer, but he was soon making enough excess money to help Daud build a proper church.

At Christmas, Amir and Elias played two of the three holy kings and got to show the children how to herd some sheep the Bahrainis had imported as gifts. In February, it was sixty degrees and didn't snow at all.

The week before his seventy-second birthday, Amir was feeling sick. Neighbors brought him soup and bread, and Hala came to sit for an hour by his bedside.

He was happy, then. Truly.

That June, Salim brought in sixteen friends from overseas to work for his computer business that never seemed to make a single computer. And then he expanded his house to make plenty of room for all of them.

Amir called Yacoub to complain, but Yacoub was too busy in Turkey to talk to his own uncle, so Amir invited Hala over and vented to her instead.

"It's not a good thing he's doing bringing those people to Bir Qalam," Amir said. "Why does he need them? Why can't he teach people in the village to make his computers with him?"

"He doesn't make computers," said Hala. "He makes computer programs. And he brought those people because Yacoub told him to. They're a strong, creative team and they innovate better with more face time."

"They don't make computers?" said Amir. "I thought his business was in computers."

"It's a new kind of social networking," Hala said. "When people use the internet, their web browsers track where they go. Salim's company helps people find friends who have browsing patterns that might be good matches for their own."

His business was to be a matchmaker for friends? On people's computers? "I still don't think it's a good idea." Amir said. "And I don't think it's a good thing that he made his house so big when he's not even married. What's all the space for?"

Hala smiled. "You want me to tell him he should get married soon? Then why don't you play the matchmaker's matchmaker?"

"That's not my business," Amir said. "You know that's not for an old man to do."

"I was just teasing you," Hala said.

By August, Salim's friend-matching business was doing unusually well and the Bahrainis were excited about how much money they'd earned from their shares in it. They gave Yacoub a big bonus and he built a big house.

Amir called him when he found out Yacoub had given Salim's co-workers permission to make their own big houses, too.

"What are you doing?" said Amir. "Why are you giving away pieces of Bir Qalam? Are you trying to prostitute out your own home?"

"Calm down, uncle. I'm trying to watch out for the village, not destroy it," said Yacoub. "We don't have a strong economy of our own, but as long as Salim's business does well, there's hope for the future here. We can get more jobs onto the island. Or do you want the people you worked so hard to get here wander away again because there's no work?"

And of course Amir didn't. He wanted them to be together. He wanted every single one of them to stay. But he also didn't want to back down and look like an ignorant child. "Why doesn't Salim hire more people from the village, then? That's what I want to know!"

"Oh he is, uncle," said Yacoub. "We're setting up a call center."

That November, Daud came through the village passing out copies of *Time* magazine that had Salim's face on the cover and told everyone individually that Salim's company's value had more than doubled in the last month. A few dozen Tunisian workers came up to stay the winter because so many people had shares in the company and wanted to expand their houses.

Salim ordered himself a luxury car and started talking about building a road.

"What does Salim want a car here for?" asked Elias.

"I don't know," said Amir. "But maybe we should just be proud of his success. If it weren't for Salim, you know, there might not be many jobs here. Village life is no longer what it once was. You have to take so much more into account."

Elias nodded, but he didn't look entirely convinced. Amir didn't feel all the way convinced either.

By Amir's seventy-third birthday, there was a paved road down the middle of the village. Hardly anyone had moved away, and a group of Filipino maids had come in to clean some of the new, big houses. Twenty-four people came to Amir's birthday, but most of his neighbors were off shopping in Turkey.

By Amir's seventy-fourth birthday, the Bahrainis had built a luxury hotel and Daud had converted his church into a movie theater, since people got tired of taking a boat to Greece or Turkey when all they wanted was something to do in the evening. Amir liked a movie now and then, but he hated to need people to lend him money they all knew he wouldn't be able to pay back every time he wanted to see one.

Before Amir's seventy-fifth birthday, Elias decided to move back to America. He said he'd loved having the village back, but at Christmastime he had missed living near to a church. Three Filipino families moved in to Elias's little abandoned house next to Amir. When his birthday came, he celebrated with them and a few others. He cut up apples and laid them out for his guests and was embarrassed to find he had little more to offer.

A week later Yacoub, who'd been out on a business trip for the Bahrainis during the party, stopped by.

"Happy birthday to my favorite uncle!" he said, and handed Amir a cake.

But Amir didn't feel hungry enough to eat much.

Yacoub suggested he ought to get out more. Amir shrugged. Yacoub showed him some article on his phone that explained how elderly people benefitted from keeping a pet. Amir said he wasn't interested.

"Isn't there anything I can do for you?" said Yacoub.

"I don't know," said Amir. "My health is good enough." Even if his heart was not.

Yacoub shook his head. "If you need money for a trip to Turkey or something, just ask. I've done well with my partners here, and we'd have never worked so closely if it weren't for you."

Amir suppressed the annoyance he felt rising in him. Yacoub had only ever been good to him—he didn't know why his nephew reminded him now of a customer in his Greensboro shop. And yet: Yacoub's offer left him feeling both humiliated and hollow. Feeling that were familiar enough. "What is Turkey to me?" asked Amir. He tried to say it with a finality that would head off any further offers or questions, but his conviction faltered. He could dismiss Turkey easily enough, and yet—what was this strange and busy place? What had happened to Bir Qalam?

Yacoub's phone rang. He silenced it, but Amir could tell he wanted to leave. That he was only staying out of politeness or guilt.

"You brought us here, uncle," said Yacoub. "You deserve to be happy in this place. Please tell me how to help you."

Amir smiled wryly. "In a place like this, all I know how to do is work."

But Yacoub didn't understand what Amir meant. "I can help you find a job," Yacoub said. "Something to keep your mind occupied." He brightened. "Or else I could give you a little starter fund if you'd like to set up your own shop again."

And perhaps that was the only real choice. Elias was gone, and the village was being lost beneath its own rootless wealth.

What else did such a world want from Amir Mousa? "I can pay you back," Amir said. "In a few years. You've done so much for me already."

"Of course, uncle," said Yacoub. "Of course."

And so it was that Amir Mousa opened a small convenience store on the very soil his ancestors had occupied for a thousand years.

The next year was a bad one for produce, so Amir stocked mostly chips, sodas, cheap Greek beers, nearly expired packaged pitas, and other shit he could sell to the Tunisian construction guys, to Filipino house workers, and even to the occasional tight-fisted Bulgarian tourist.

To customers who'd half forgotten where they had come from and had no idea where they were going. Who lived on the shallow buzz of passing sensation, who lacked the weight in the gut of memory that grounded men like him, like Elias—or even the filthy Zionist, Fridman. He sat in his shop, idly glancing at a television set mounted in the corner and ringing up customers who would never know what it meant to really belong somewhere.

And who could never in their lifetimes hope to feel an anguish and a sense of loss quite like his.

SOJOURNERS

A KALEIDOSCOPE OF VERY SHORT STORIES ABOUT MIGRANTS
BASED ON THE JEWISH LITURGICAL CALENDAR

Passover
Exodus

By the time Martin woke up, the Angel of Death had already come and gone, leaving precious little behind. Grandmother was dead and Martin's mother was dead; Martin's father had already been dead for some time. Muzinga was dead and Martin's other sister was missing, perhaps dead, and Martin guessed by the large bloody scab on the back of his head that he was meant to be dead, too.

Half the village had been burned, and the other half was quiet except for the sounds of insects, who never surrendered their noisy approach to existence in good times or bad, by day or by night. A few soldiers were dead, and the rest had presumably moved on, although who was to say whether they might come back?

Martin didn't think they would. It seemed to him that even the ghosts of his ancestors had been killed that day and that there was nothing, truly nothing for anyone to return for.

And so Martin, the firstborn son of dead parents from a dead world, left forever.

Shavuot
Stones

I had a dream last night where the pagans were right so every hill river grove had its own god and its own law and you belonged wholly to the place where you lived and when you moved it was like uprooting yourself and being tossed aching exposed stinging in the air until you found a new place to grow over you like ivy or kudzu so that you belonged to it instead and its god filled in the cavity that was supposed to be your heart and its law grew out of your ears and eyes in hungry blooming clusters.

But then someone wrote on two stones, and my roots grew into the spaces where he'd carved the words. And I swore then and I've kept it since, that those words would be home for me everywhere.

The 9th of Av
Balbir Singh Sodhi

The flowers were white, soft-petalled, I don't know the name but they smelled like morning and they made us forget, for a moment, the smell of spilled gas all around, and exhaust, and the heat of this crazy concrete jungle we built in the desert.

The petals were soft like the soil he'd brought in—not like this hard Arizona stuff—soft, loose, dark soil he'd brought in from somewhere else, and his hands worked through it while he planted.

His turban was blue that day. And the blood was red.

And the gunshot had been loud, so loud and so sudden.

Rosh Hashana
Shaadi Aj Kal

They had met, of course, and talked it over. Their families approved, but these days things are more complicated than that; they had to decide for themselves if it was all right, and he had to hope she was telling the truth, a question which troubled him (the last girl had felt pressured but kept her mouth shut, and then broken the engagement after everything had been arranged.)

She was a Dhaliwal from Doraha. Among other things, Uncle pointed out, Doraha was home to Ludhiana's first McDonald's and their famous McAloo sandwich. Never mind that, scolded Auntie, Gurmit's wife Baljit had also been a Dhaliwal from Doraha and she was so kind and danced so well at weddings and parties.

He was a Gill from Delano, California and was sticking to a farmer's life. With his father, he grew grapes and peaches and walnuts, and his mother kept a little garden close by with different varieties of spice. He didn't wear a turban, and he'd cut his hair, but other than that, he was all right.

The ring ceremony went well, and the wedding was quite memorable and touching, even though the same two uncles got drunk and had the same fight as at every wedding for the past fifteen years.

It wasn't until he picked her up at the airport nearly a month later, after the snafus had been cleared up and the paperwork finished just right, that they realized the

Day of Judgment was upon them. Their marriage would be good, everyone was confident—but privately the two of them, sitting next to each other on the long drive home, wondered if it would also be sweet, sweet like the fruits of the tree which was then casting its long shadow into the room they'd share that night.

Yom Kippur
Kol Nidre

Abuela, whose grave I had promised to always visit—I'm sorry.

That garden plot, mother, I told you as a child I would tend when you got old and your joints turned hard—whisper my apologies to the weeds.

My wife, who can't go see her sister at her wedding, in case she somehow wouldn't be able to make it back past immigration—forgive me.

Mijo, I said you would have it better than me, but now—we'll see.

My father, who prepared me to live in a world he didn't know was disappearing— have I disappointed you?

Ernesto, who wanted to go through the best and worst with me—if you have a steady one, could you send me your address?

Everyone who is still somewhere, every sun that rises over my old home and does not see me, every drop of rain God sends to nourish crops I haven't sown—what happened to the life I'd thought I would lead?

All vows, all the vows I didn't dream I wouldn't be able to keep—please, please, release me.

Sukkot
Snow

He loved it at first—the dazzling endlessness of it, the abundance, the unexpectedness, the sheer *novelty* excited him; this was nothing like the places he came from and it gave him an overwhelming sense of peace the first time he stared out the window at this strange new world that seemed to have fallen all at once, fully formed, from the sky. He imagined himself walking out into its vast whiteness and forgetting his refugee's past entirely, his life as blank and pure and open as his surroundings.

But now, Martin hated the snow. He hated the unfamiliar cold, a cold bitter enough to withstand even the rare hours of direct sunlight. He hated the precarious walk, between the hours of four and four-thirty, from his run-down apartment to the bus stop on Cleveland Avenue and he hated feeling hurt, embarrassed, and alone the many times he fell flat on his back.

It broke his heart to watch his very breath freeze and fall as he wandered the city, looking for more work. And he cried when the snow bent his head down by falling in sheets all around him, just as he cried tears of frustration when the falling stopped and the light came again and the terrible glare made him wish himself blind, a blind stranger in a strange and snow-covered land.

Simchat Torah
Bhangra

Supu and Rajan set up the speakers on the back porch while Devinder Uncle looked out over his farm. He had done well for himself, here. Organic certification had meant relative security from the politics between small farmers and big packers, plus a niche market that was willing to pay for quality. He'd been able to care for his parents in their old age. None of his children had gotten into drugs, and his grandchildren were beautiful and full of promise. The government wasn't looking for anyone he knew here, and no one he knew was looking for trouble with the government, either.

So why did he miss the Punjab he'd left so much? He knew, of course, that it was gone: the rivers polluted beyond recognition in the name of so-called progress, the neighbors gone to Canada and Kenya, to Yorkshire and Yuba City. And he knew all too well about the intermittent political disaster he'd watched for decades across the distance of two oceans and the closeness of blood.

But could Devinder ever leave Punjab as completely as his Scythian ancestors, before they became Jats, had packed up and left the drought-prone steppes of Central Asia, working now as mercenaries, now as herders and farmers until they found a place for their families to live? Could he turn the page so easily from his childhood in a homeland to his adulthood in migration, tell himself that so long as his family was intact and there was room on God's earth for them, he still had a home?

He didn't know. But he still danced tonight as the speakers shook the ground with the beat of the dhol in so many strange remixes, and he danced into the morning when they turned the speakers off and sang improvised lyrics and clapped and laughed together like they used to, like they'd done so many years ago in the village when he left.

Hanukah
Light

When Judah Maccabee returned to Jerusalem illegally and undocumented, he knew that sooner or later there might well be hell to pay. After all, he was an ardent opponent of English-only policies, like his father had been, and sooner or later an attention-drawing altercation was bound to occur. Then it would be back to the mountains for Judah, who made a point of traveling light, back like Pancho Villa giving General Pershing the slip, and it would be farewell again to the warmth of this kitchen table and conversations with his wife and the children she had borne him here.

Maybe Judah looked out into this night, ruled only by the new moon, and wished just once to give up all difference forever, that he could bleach his skin and bend his voice and bow to all the local idols just for the sake of peace.

But Judah lit the candles anyway, and he put them in his window.

Purim
Haman's Prize

In his dream, Martin saw the judge from immigration court. A group of immigration officers in uniform came up and asked him what he planned on doing with

Martin, and he told them it was time for America to send Martin home. Martin felt a bone-crushing heaviness then, felt himself buried under a pile of papers so deep that the pressure alone made it impossible for him to draw a breath, though his mouth and nose could feel the fullness and the promise of the air. Then Martin felt himself drowning in the papers, as they surrounded him like the waters of the Lukuga one night so many years ago, looser now but all around him, filling his vision, making his movements slow and awkward, directionless—filtering out all the light, dizzying him until he could no longer distinguish up from down. Finally, someone set the papers on fire, and once again Martin emerged as half his village burned.

Then the dream changed again and the papers were gone. The judge stood in Martin's village, now, while Martin watched from across an indifferent ocean. The judge stood alone, and surprised. The village was an empty void, of course, but the judge still had to stand there: more alone than he had ever been in his life, though surrounded by a thousand hungry soldiers with gleaming wild eyes that bore into him with the chaotic logic of undirected revenge.

TALES OF TEANCUM SINGH ROSENBERG

1

THEY SAY he wanted to be a weaver, like Kabir, but developed an inexplicable allergy to thread. No matter, he said, that part was all metaphor anyway: what he really wanted to weave together were the fragments of stories that had been kept in corners and boxes, fragments that hung in the air or got stuck between the teeth at dinner. And so he wove, sometimes by day and especially by night, and produced great rugs and tapestries, both for living people and as tributes to the Singularity of God.

It was only when he hung them outside that he realized they were all written in a language no one spoke. He was devastated.

One day he complained to God, said "Why did you make my mind a loom—was it only for this?"

Some say God began to answer him slowly, and the words filled the rest of his years. Others say God didn't answer at all for a long time, until quite suddenly at the end.

But how shall I begin to tell you the stories he lived? How can I express what they mean to us? As Herschel of Ostropol to the Ashkenazim, as Nasreddin Hodja to the Turks, so is Teancum Singh Rosenberg to my people. He is less wise, perhaps, and certainly less witty, but he is ours.

He's a fool, he's a folktale, he's a broken half of a hero. He may or may not have even ever existed, but his tales are still our language, and for someone's sake, our language ought to be spoken, ought to be stored in books and kept for a day when somewhere it's desperately needed.

Accounts of his childhood are most likely retroactive creations, projected back after people began to tell stories about him out of a need (like mine) for some sort of beginning. Because of this, they are improbable and often contradictory.

In this sense, they are entirely typical of childhood sketches.

One account has it that his home was an idyllic paradise—until he was born. The first thing the infant Rosenberg did was to shake his fist at the sky itself, and the next thing the sky did was to cover itself in grey so as not to have to witness his insolence.

The sky remained grey for nearly two years, until the child began to speak and cursed it; the sky responded by pouring down unceasing rain to drown out Rosenberg's words.

When, after some time, the ground realized that the rain and drudgery had been sent on the child's account, it begged the sky to take them back. The sky consented, leaving Teancum's father's farm to wither and dry until it blew away.

Perhaps there is some truth to the story, and that is why our only homeland is the wind.

In another version, Teancum's parents quarreled bitterly even before his birth. His father alternated between periods of indignation, righteous or otherwise, and deep depressions. His mother, on the other hand, was quick to apologize for her own temper—but just as quick to remember during the course of her apologies what had made her so angry in the first place and burst into a heat of rage again.

If his parents were loving and good during the day, they tore the house in half fighting at night. If they were loving and kind at night, they tore the house into hundredths during the day.

If Teancum himself was often torn in halves or hundredths in the course of these fights, that may serve to explain something about his later nature.

Perhaps it because of the way he was torn that we still tell fragments of stories about him.

The clues Teancum Singh Rosenberg gives us about his own childhood are as follows:

When one host asked why he tended to eat so quickly and how he had become so generally itinerant, wandering forever from place to place, Teancum Singh replied: "As a child, I had to fight with dogs for my scraps. I've kept the scraps, so somewhere inside of me the dogs remain also."

A mother of one child and a father of another were talking in a courtyard once—mourning the damage their poor skills as parents would no doubt do to their children's minds and souls. Overhearing them, Rosenberg remarked: "Half-broken children grow up wanting to heal the world. Why raise a child whole and content? All it will want to do is amuse itself and eat."

Once, a conspiracy against his life forced Teancum Singh into hiding. He avoided harm, he told a friend, by playing games with a group of four-year-olds—though three times their size, he was otherwise too much like them to be detected.

So much for the enigma of his beginnings. Accounts agree that as he aged, Teancum Singh Rosenberg was given two gifts from God: the loom of his mind, and the aching desire to fill it with the stories of the past, woven into an aid and protection for the present. Searching for that help, we search through his stories. And yet it is *his* desperate search for stories that fills the oldest stories about him.

They say he would have given his thumb to learn the story of Eklavya. He would have let a worm bore through his leg without crying out to learn of Karna's fate. He would have gone by night, risking the wrath of the Emperor, to take the head of Tegh Bahadur if that meant he could hear one more tale of Gobind Singh.

He would have traded his home and wealth, if necessary, for the record of Nephi. Gone mute through life just to know what happened to Korihor. Hidden in a cavity of a rock for Ether's story's sake.

If the Messiah himself had come, Teancum Singh might have asked him to wait just a little longer while Teancum finished memorizing the legends of the Zugot and the Tannaim. How could you receive His Coming without some stories that tell you He will Come?

"Sometimes a story is a key, and the lock and the treasure chest are missing," he said. "All the more reason to gather the keys, and quickly!"

For three years, Teancum Singh Rosenberg refused to cut his hair.

"The son of two lions should know how it feels to look like one" he said.

The Huma is a bird that always flies, but almost never lands, a bird which one cannot catch even in dreams. They say, though, that whoever can touch even the shadow the flying Huma casts wrests the rule of a kingdom from destiny's hands.

They also say that Teancum Singh was listening to his grandmother tell a story when the Huma flew by. Some say the

Huma even circled him, but he stayed still and listened, even when the shadow came within the reach of his hands.

Why not chase the Huma? Why not take the time even to reach out his arm? He could have used the power, and any accompanying protection. We could have used it—even the memory of someone else's success can inspire. But—no. His hand stayed still, the shadow passed.

"Why chase after a kingdom," he said, "when in every old woman's shadow are worlds without end?"

"The scraps that I fought for," he once said "were the traditions of my ancestors.

"And oh, how the dogs fought to take them from me! How hard they tried to tear them to pieces!"

Once, Teancum studied the names of his ancestors with such *intensity* that the prophet Elijah was forced to come personally on his chariot of fire to ask him to stop: Rosenberg had drawn so much of Elijah's spirit to himself that there was little left for the rest of the world. Not wanting to disobey a prophet, Teancum Singh obeyed, but, being unwilling to surrender the intensity of his study, channeled the energy into chasing after Elijah's chariot instead, determined to follow him back to heaven itself.

Teancum followed the chariot one mile, and then twain, at which point it crossed a river that was the gateway into heaven. But the river was swift as well as deep and wide.

Teancum cried out, "Elijah, wait! How do I get to the other side?"

Over the water came Elijah's laughter back. "You are on the other side," was all he said.

"We never know who we are," said Teancum, "because we never understand God.

"And yet He is always wrapped in our history, always hiding underneath our skin."

Another time, Teancum announced that he would visit the Temple in Jerusalem. When others heard of his plan, they scoffed—said, "What wealth is in the House of Rosenberg that he could journey over an ocean?" Said, "He would have to walk, and you can't walk on water with such heavy, callused feet."

Rosenberg only smiled. Later, he took off his shoes, covered his head, and whispered to Baruch Moroni Brar, "The Wailing Wall must serve as both the Western and the Eastern bounds now. We all stand in the Temple, but how rarely do we recognize its Holy Ground!"

Most often, he freely admitted himself to be blind to it. "I was born less to see," he said, "than to remember that there was once a story in which someone saw.

"And, if Drona doesn't keep me from it, to share the story of that old story's half-forgotten existence."

Every quest requires obstacles, and Drona was Teancum Singh's greatest. Or perhaps it was the other was around: Drona's was the quest, and Teancum Singh was a pebble in the path, a would-be obstacle who went almost entirely without notice.

They met only once, though they shared the small-seeming space of a single world. It is, therefore, impossible to understand Teancum Singh Rosenberg without knowing something about Drona. One of the things we most desperately want from Teancum is for him to prove Newton's laws by being Drona's reactive opposite, though we understand that our Teancum was never Drona's equal. How could anyone compare with the latter's influence? Some say the spirit of Drona still fills the earth.

If Teancum is a spark in the darkness, Drona is the moonless night. And why should the night notice just one spark? If Teancum is a freshwater fish, Drona is the ocean, and there is always room in the ocean for one more fish's corpse.

If Drona is a vast warship, though, Teancum is a leak, and in that, at least, we take hope.

They were both teachers. Teancum was a teacher with few or no pupils; Drona's students were drawn from every land. Teancum's lessons were like a hole in the pocket; Drona's could line the pockets with gold—he had always been known as a master of craft. Almost every craft.

"There are few skills he hasn't mastered," said Rosenberg on a particularly bitter occasion, "Two of those, unfortunately, are mercy and truth."

Few cared to listen to Rosenberg for long unless all other alternatives had been exhausted. The perceptive and the ambitious, the leaders of today and the leaders of tomorrow, flocked to Drona and hoped to touch his feet.

"Nothing makes me feel so sick," Teancum said, "as remembering that Drona will rule this world for longer than you or I can hope to live."

Would Drona have recognized himself in the Weaver's accusation? He was, after all, never acknowledged as a leader in the world, but rather as the servant of the leaders. And he would have felt bound, even in the absence of leaders, to his sense of duty to a certain view of the world.

"Even Drona lives under Drona's thumb" Teancum is known to have complained. "Even Drona is darkened by Drona's shadow."

What did Drona know best? The martial disciplines, with their pursuit of pure excellence. The discipline of duty as an ethic, duty that pre-empted further exploration of right and wrong. What did Drona know? How to serve Kauravas and to serve Pandavas as if they were Kauravas; to instill in the Pandavas through his devotion an arrogance that made them act like Kauravas. "If good and evil were cousins," said Teancum Singh, "Drona will try to make them brothers.

"If they are brothers, he would try to convince us that they are one and the same."

Would Drona have assigned himself such intent, any intent? His role was not to propagate any new view, but to perpetuate an existing order. Drona is a symbol of order—an order in which we do not and cannot fit.

"In these days of Drona, our choice is to starve or else be devoured. In the days of Drona, the dogs are no different than princes and kings" Teancum said. When pressed for evidence of these claims, he offered the following:

"How did Eklavya gain Drona's notice? He shot the mouth of a dog shut."

And yet it was the mouths of our ancestors and not the mouths of the dogs which were closed. So often our mouths are closed out of habit still, and it is to this impulse that the Weaver Rosenberg speaks.

"You should say the Truth," he said. "The Truth should be spoken in our tongue, in every tongue! Never mind what happened to Mansur!"

Friends told him to be careful. Friends warned him against likewise attracting Drona's attention, of making him feel a duty to punish Teancum Singh as he had Eklavya.

They advised him, above all, to show a certain outward respect for the status quo. If you speak the truth, they said, do so softly.

"You can push the envelope, Teancum" said one woman, "but gently, so you don't make a noise by tearing through its edge."

"I want to break through the envelope" he said, "and then turn back and set it on fire."

His friends thought he went too far saying so, tempted himself and fate.

They were right.

"The Prophets are my witnesses" said Rosenberg, "God and Drona have never seen the world in anything like the same way."

"To Drona, the world simply *is.*" And the Prophets—what do they say? "They show the world as God's story: unfolding, surprising, a story within a story without beginning or end."

Sometimes pieces of that story upset him.

Baruch Moroni Brar records that Teancum once took off his shoes, covered his head, and unrolled another page of the earth, which is a scroll. He wept then, and Baruch asked why. Rosenberg replied that he would have sworn and yelled instead, but that he was trying to act like the God in whose presence we all stand.

(After noting the incident, Brar emphasizes that whichever page we find ourselves standing on, we must not forget that when this world ends, the scroll will be rolled up again.)

Another time Teancum is said to have witnessed a miracle in the desert: a rock turned into bread. He then asked God to show him a second miracle, and turn the bread into rock again so that he, like Jacob, would have a place to lay his head.

Why are we drawn to these stories of Teancum, even when they makes the least sense? Perhaps because the role of the protagonist in folktales is to mediate reality, sometimes even by stepping outside of it.

Especially by stepping outside of it, if only to show us that such a space exists.

2

It happened once that Rabbi Eliezer, Rabbi Yehoshua, Rabbi Elazar ben Azaryah, Rabbi Akiva and Rabbi Tarphon were in the same Sunday school one week. Teancum Singh was late.

When he arrived, they were discussing the nature of prophetic reliability.

Rabbi Eliezer said "Only when two or more prophets speak the same truth can it be considered equal to a word of the Lord. As it is written, 'whether by mine own voice or the voice of my servants, it is the same.' 'Servants,' not 'servant.' When a prophet speaks alone, he may speak as a man, but when he speaks with the intent and witness of another prophet, their words are surely Ha-Shem's."

Rabbi Tarphon, however, said "It is also written, 'whatsoever they shall speak when moved by the Holy Ghost shall be scripture.' That is, even the words of a prophet speaking alone are surely of the Lord when he is moved."

Rabbi Ben Azaryah said, "I am like a man of seventy years old, and yet I could not succeed in interpreting this scripture until Ben Zoma explained it to me. 'Moved by the Holy Ghost' means the Prophet cannot remain the same, he must be moved to speak against his natural prejudice and inclinations. Only then are his words surely also the Lord's words. Otherwise, the counsel is binding but the perfection uncertain."

Rabbi Akiva then said, "What does the saying mean, that the Prophet will never lead the people astray? Is it not written, 'all we like sheep have gone astray.'? 'We' is the people, 'All we'—this includes the prophets. And it is also written, 'The beauty of Israel is slain upon thy high places: how are the mighty fallen!' It is possible, then, for a Prophet, also, to break faith, for a Prophet, also, to fall."

Teancum Singh answered, and said, "The Prophet can never lead the church away from the Lord because a Prophet can never escape the Lord. As it was in the days of Jonah, so it is in the last days: even a disobedient Prophet does not cease to be a Prophet, and even his rebellion is swallowed up into the purpose of Ha-Shem. A prophet is bound to the Lord, even cursed with Him: as it is written, 'the burden of the word of the Lord.'

"God will forge every prophet into his Story."

And so he searched again for stories, believing in their potential and malleability, in both their absolute and relative significance. He knocked on the doors, begging people for stories. He knocked on the doors even of abandoned houses, inhabited only by ghosts.

Why did he search, again and again, forgoing meals and abandoning shelters?

"The only way to see this world clearly is to see it from all the different worlds inside of it. That is why only God will ever see this world clearly," he said.

On a certain kind of story: "I don't remember history to avoid repeating it—I know I will repeat it; I am not afraid of repeating it—perhaps this time I will notice the hidden treasures, the unexpected possibilities for healing."

"We move through stories, we love through stories, mothers give birth to children but we have to clothe them in stories or they will freeze in this cold."

"Stories are my meat and drink today" he said. "Stories are this night's shelter."

Another time Teancum said, "Every movement must have its parables—even Shiva couldn't move the world without the parable of his dance."

"Without stories to move us, we are doomed to stay the same. That is why Drona and his servants hate the stories I search for. But the loss of every story shrinks the world: does he really want the world to be so small that there will only be room a single eye?"

"The dogs know I am looking for the scraps they still wish to tear. The swine know I am looking for lost pearls.

"But who am I to stop? Even if they turn and tear me, who am I to stop this gathering I take part in?"

He had sworn to go to the ends of the earth gathering stories, but his quest took him also to the center. Knowing what the consequences might be, he went and studied in a school that took Drona's image as its Guru as part of his search for a certain story.

When Drona found out, of course, he shut the school down. But not before demanding payment. Teancum offered his thumb, as is customary, but Drona said, "I already have Eklavya's.

"My price is your tongue."

The Weaver Rosenberg shook with rage. Never had he so desperately wished to put a javelin through someone's heart.

After Drona demanded his tongue, Rosenberg went into a deep depression. He couldn't speak, of course, and the silence was like the Underworld to him.

Perversely, rumors began to spread at that time that the silence had given Rosenberg enlightenment, or that his deep mediations had endowed him with mystical powers.

The only power he ever claimed, in any case, was invisibility.

"The secret," he is said to have written, "is this: learn to see your soul through another mortal's eyes."

One scrap of his writing from this time has survived, though it may well be a corrupted copy of an earlier document, or else an outright forgery. The scrap includes this line:

"Oh Lord God deliver me in thy due time from the little narrow prison almost as it were total darkness of paper pen and ink and its crooked broken scattered and imperfect language"

He slept more often then, though fitfully, slept half the day and half the night in restless little snatches.

He dreamed, then, more than usual, they say, and it pained him terribly not to be able to speak the dreams to those around him.

When awake, he often behaved as though a madman. He pushed rocks up hills and watched them roll down again. He moved into the desert, ate locusts, planted a gourd for shade and then stopped watering it and let the sun scorch his skin.

And yet, some stories say, he was also often coherent and kind when he was awake in those days. Did work for others that was physically demanding and thankless, perhaps trying to wear himself out for his next battle with morning and night, perhaps desperate to keep alive his surviving sense of purpose.

Perhaps he did it to feel whole. Even the broken sometimes feel their wholeness. Somehow, Teancum Singh carried on.

Did he ever truly despair, ever resent all that he had lived for?

Yes. At least one time.

Some say the silence drove him to it, made him feel as if there were too much trapped under his skin. Others say he was simply tired, and that he likely would have grown tired in any case.

They agree that once, though, he lost the will even to be himself.

In a certain city, he had heard, people who wanted or needed extra time could purchase it from a certain craftsman called the Time-Blower. The Time-Blower would take old, used, unwanted time and draw it out of the bodies of those who wanted themselves lightened of it, then work it in a forge and blow it into shapes for every occasion.

In his storefront, there were round, dense, dark pieces of time for people who needed to catch up on sleep. There were double-edged pieces on display he blew specially for people to make up missed appointments. The Time-Blower also crafted cavernous clear pieces for people who just needed time to think and squatter, squarish pieces for people to work in. He blew old time into wings for people who wanted to have fun, and hung them right above his window. He made long, curved tubes for children trying to reach a certain age more quickly and kept them in a case behind the counter at the back.

When Teancum approached the Time-Blower and scrawled him a message saying what he had come for, he was ushered out of the storefront and back through an alley to a separate entrance. He heard a drunkard moan. "I think you took more than I'd already forgotten...I told you, I only wanted to lose what I'd been lost for." The Time-Blower mumbled a quick apology, but the drunk just grunted, then rolled over and fell asleep.

"How much?" asked the Time-Blower.

Rosenberg motioned for paper and pen. "Everything," he wrote. "It might take a while. The time I keep inside is deeper than I've lived for."

And they say the Time-Blower's eyes got big and hungry when he took his first real look at the size of Teancum's veins, thick dark cables that marked their course visibly like river-maps on his skin. The Time-Blower tried his biggest and fastest needles first, then worked his way down to his daintiest and most delicate ones—but every time he'd get the needle in to suck the old time out, the vein would collapse. Sixteen times he tried, until Teancum's arms were riddled with barren holes and the Time-Blower's hand ached, but nothing flowed out at all.

Teancum Singh got up and left then.

He was no prophet, but he had his own burden from the Lord.

3

Years of silence taught Teancum, again, how to sleep. He learned a new serenity, one that requires neither reconciliation with nor rejection of things as they are, only patience with the paradox.

He ate consistently again for the first time since he'd lost his tongue, training himself to remember tastes he could no longer experience instead of recoiling at the loss of what our people accept as one of mankind's most significant senses, the sense that gives us memories of home and family, a sense that most clearly approximates our souls' ability for longing.

He took, against his former habit, to rising very early, and tried to feel the way Guru Nanak's singing of Japji still hangs in the ambrosial predawn air.

The world went on without his voice or noticeable influence. Sometimes good, compromised and disfigured almost beyond recognition, triumphed over evil. Sometimes evil triumphed over a few broken fragments of good and then gradually lost force, decaying from active evil into little more than residual momentum.

Tens of thousands were born; tens of thousands died.

Then hundreds of thousands, thousands of thousands, died in the battle at Kurukshetra.

Kurukshetra.

The very name hangs in the air when spoken; it is a heavy incantation. It summons the smells of charred bodies, sights of death and broken weapons, cataclysmic, mindless slaughter. Did wrong triumph? Did right triumph? We hardly remember; the battle lasted so long, so many last screams long.

Geologists say that limestone is made from compressed biological matter; it is the stone of the once-living. At Kurukshetra you could dig through a foot of human lime.

They say in the battle, one man ate another's heart in revenge. A perfectly honest man told a lie. A warrior whose identity rested only in his sense of duty had doubts, hesitated to strike. A son of the sun, of the morning, fell—forgetting the words that might have saved him. A land that had been holy was drowned in blood, and when the moon rose at night it was also covered in it.

Half the world died, and Drona died with it.

Baruch Moroni Brar had been there, but survived.

He called Teancum Singh to come salvage something from the carnage.

Kurukshetra and Cumorah—why is meaning so often hidden under land known for the meaningless? Why are the Golden

Plates always hidden under the site of a ghallugara, a holocaust?

At Kurukshetra, Teancum Singh spoke to men's bones, gathered their stories just before they became dust. He spoke to the dust, gathered stories that had lived in men's bones.

How? How did he speak after so many years of such painful silence?

They say that on Drona's corpse he found and reclaimed his own tongue.

"Once I had wished to kill him for his evil," said Rosenberg, "but every evil has a brother—you could kill the world before evil was stopped.

"And before you could finish," he said, "evil would find you in its line of succession. Perhaps I am evil's brother, too."

They say he gathered Drona's story, and was taken aback by its beauty. Saw that there was a kind of honesty even in Drona's most brutal betrayals. Saw how Drona, in turn, had been betrayed—by his best-loved pupils, and more deeply still by the very order he had believed in, the very order that is still perpetuated in his name.

They say that passages of the story were so harrowing that they could never be written, only spoken, and that other passages, more moving still, could never be spoken, only sung, and that the most moving passage could only be prayed.

They say he turned to the future to gather our stories, then…and prayed we'd have the strength to live them.

THE TRIAL OF AL-MANSUR

THREE DAYS after Rashid al-Mansur opened the gates of his treasury to the Khanate's officers and was compelled once again to show them the emptiness of each vault, his slaves met in council.

Musa spoke first, and for justice:

"I would to God," he said, "that we had no need to assemble this night. I would to God fortune still smiled on the House of Mansur. But when a day of reckoning comes, our duty is to sit in judgment on the covenant. In these dark times, bad counsel has sapped the strength of the body—so for our children's sake we must seek the proper cure.

"God is my witness that I know the love each of you feels for our Master. I know how each of you treasures the day your fate was first bound with salt and blood at the altar to the name of al-Mansur. And I've seen the sweat you've spent from year to year to honor the salt of that covenant. Has any of us been unfaithful in his labors or careless in his craft? Haven't we punished all the liars and the frauds and the drunkards who made a mock of their promise?

"But after all our years of faith, where is the peace of the dove-offering? Twice now the coffers have been empty. Twice the bread of age withheld from our brothers and our own rations diminished. The honor that once rested on our House is fled, and the marketplaces no longer grant trust to the word of an agent of Mansur.

"Shall we wait, brothers, until we are all clothed in rags, until we are bowed down with age and broken with hunger? Shall we press on in our labors until we are begging instead of trading in our Master's name? Until reputable merchants bar their doors against our coming?"

"I would to God—" said Musa, and then he fell silent for a moment.

"I have never wished harm to our Master," he said, "but justice and reason alike demand his own blood now at the altar. And so this night we must agree to give voice to that demand. As is our right. As is our duty to the promises."

Ibrahim spoke next, and for mercy:

"It is true that the life of Rashid al-Mansur is forfeit. Surely he can hear how old men's empty stomachs cry out as witnesses against him, surely each empty coffer beckons to him now as though it were his tomb. Our Master is a man of honor. If we choose it, he will accept a just death without complaint.

"But can we have justice only by blood? The covenant is still ours to make demands through—or offer pardon by. Once before, we chose to save our Master by releasing him from promises he made when he was young and full of strength, and with the help of our sacrifices he led the House back out of emptiness for a time. But perhaps we still expect him to provide more than a good man can wrest from the markets for his slaves in these days of darkness.

"In the name of God the Merciful, let us offer mercy to our master. And then let us pray to God the Beneficent that good counsel and renewal may again shine over al-Mansur."

Shahid spoke next, and of hunger. Rahim spoke of hope. And then Akil and Abdel spoke and argued at length about money and markets and gambles and odds.

The council pressed on past midnight.

At the other end of the compound, Rashid al-Mansur sat by an open window under the light of a waning crescent moon and wept.

"Don't be afraid, Father," said his son, Malik. "Your death would bring them nothing. It must be difficult for their pride, but they can see reason. They will alter the terms of the covenant again to save the House they take shelter in."

"I don't weep for my death," said Rashid. "I weep because for all I thought I had built up, today I have only a tarnished name and an empty estate for your inheritance."

"How could you have any more when your slaves have eaten so much up?" growled Malik. "They take the bread of age from your hand—as if they had no children to support them! Your laborers stand by old customs that slow our work at the docks and in the warehouses; your agents refuse to learn enough about foreigners to win their contracts, so they come back again and again with only wind in their hands. And still they aren't ashamed to live well—"

"They live," said Rashid, "by what I promised them. Never more. For these past four years, less."

"It is too much," said Malik. "The old promises offer too much for old work in a new world."

"But my son," said Rashid. "I didn't buy their work. I bought them. And if the world changed, why didn't I prepare them for it?"

"You did everything you could for them," said Malik. "More than enough."

"Then why have I reduced them to sitting in a council of the covenant again?" Rashid said.

In the streets, a stray dog howled. Rashid turned away from his son and looked up toward the moon once more.

"The day will come," said Malik, "when we do away with the covenants. When hired servants do a merchant's labors and aging slaves no longer hang like a millstone around his neck."

Rashid thought of the smoke that went up from the altar on the day he offered sacrifices for Halim, Falah, Khalid—the first three slaves he inherited from his own father. He thought of the gentleness in Halim's eyes, the intelligence he saw in Falah and the fierce loyalty that was apparent even then in Khalid. He had failed them. He had failed all of them, every last slave in al-Mansur. And now the House would die—either because they would demand it of him, or else because they would offer him another chance to save it and he still would not know how.

"That insight is my inheritance," said Malik. "With hired servants, I can bring our family wealth again. I can make a place for us in a new world."

Rashid looked down at his hands. Perhaps Malik was right. Perhaps the marketplaces were too crowded, too vast, too volatile for oaths of lifetime fidelity today. Perhaps Rashid's sense of honor itself was just another weight around his son's neck.

Malik heard the footsteps on the stairs first. Rashid only noticed them because his son's head had turned.

Musa brought the scroll with the slaves' decision and laid it reverently at his Master's feet. And for Rashid, the seal was like a kiss and the swirling script a hundred last embraces and the sentence of death was a sweet relief.

THE MAULANA AZAD MEMORIAL LAMPPOST
OF PANIPATNAM

IF YOU were to ask me when, exactly, the pain started or how it was, precisely, that I at first failed to notice my urine changing from its usual light yellow to an alarming shade of red, I'd be hard-pressed to tell you; if you were to ask me on what day I was admitted to the hospital, or who drove me there, I'd draw a blank. The only element of the first week of my stay, in fact, which I can recall with any degree of accuracy, is what the anesthesiologist, Dr. John Kumar, told me as I was drifting off into his drug-induced sleep.

"Count to ten," he said.

"One," I said, and thought of the disarray I'd left on my desk, wondering if I'd ever see it again.

"Two," I said, and wondered about the hospital I'd been born in, and whether the walls had the same shade of blue as the ones here.

"Three, Four, Five," I said, and remembered, for no reason, what my uncle had told me when I was only ten years old about the terrible reign of Belgium's King Leopold II over the Congo.

"Six," I said, and remembered that my car was desperately in need of an oil change.

"Seven," I said, and thought of how my grandfather had been a plane mechanic for the navy during World War Two.

"Eight, Nine," I said, and realized that I no longer felt my body's terrible pain.

"Ten," I said, and didn't know what else to think about.

"That's odd" said Dr. Kumar. "You're not supposed to actually reach ten."

I don't like it when doctors say "that's odd." It's unprofessional, not to mention unsettling. I think the Hippocratic oath should be revised to explicitly ban phrases like that.

"Can you see my face?" said Dr. Kumar.

"Except for the part covered with a mask—yes, I can." I said.

"That's quite odd," said Dr. Kumar. "Close your eyes. Can you still see my face?"

"Of course," I said.

"Can you see the ceiling of this room?"

"Yes, now that you mention it, I can."

"Can you see the surgeon's instruments on that table over there?"

I shuddered. "Yes. I can see everything you tell me."

"Really?" said Dr. Kumar. "That's quite interesting. Can you see the moon's reflection in the scalpel?"

It was at once terrifying and beautiful.

"Can you see the leprechaun-shaped scar about a quarter-inch above the surgeon's eyebrow?"

I swore that it was smirking at me. "Yes, I see it."

"Can you see the monster under your bed?"

His chest rose and fell in a sickly, uneven pattern, and he seemed to have a bad case of pinkeye. His fur was falling out in patches, and in a few of the bald places there was a strange scabbing on his skin, probably from some sort of fungus. He shivered violently in the hygienic cold of the operating room. I felt myself becoming overwhelmed with nausea. "Yes, I can see. I can see."

"Fascinating. Can you see into my heart?"

The nausea receded as I focused on the way the soothing green of Dr. Kumar's scrubs gave way to the brown of his chest, then the pale yellow-white of his tendons, the grayish-white of his bones, and the deep purple of his heart. Tiny letters and diagrams were tattooed in ever-so-fine print all along it, but, out of a desire to be a good patient and follow my doctor's directions precisely, I ignored them and looked around at the aorta, the pulmonary veins and arteries, and even the thick, pulsing surface of the left ventricle to find a way to peer inside the heart.

And then, all at once, I was simply there in the muggy warmth and blackness of it.

"Can you see it?" said Dr. Kumar.

"I'm quite sure I'm there, but I can't *see* anything yet," I told him.

"Isn't there any light?" he said.

As a matter of fact, there wasn't. Or was there? Yes, there, in the distance I could make it out: an ancient and frail-looking lamppost. And there, under it, a young boy with a book and skin even darker than Dr. Kumar's.

"Who's the boy under the lamppost?" I said.

"He's reading a book?"

"Yes."

"And his brow is furrowed? As if he's reading with great intensity?"

"Yes."

"And the air around you is warm and dark?"

"Like a night in the tropics."

Dr. Kumar sighed. "That's my father," he said. "I was afraid he'd gotten in there."

"Scalpel" said a voice from somewhere far out in the sky.

"What's going on?" I said.

"Oh, I don't think you want to see that," said Dr. Kumar.
"Shall I tell you a story instead?"
"Tell me anything," I said.
And so it was that he did.

"My paternal grandfather born was a *dalit*, one of the untouchable caste, in what is now the state of Andhra Pradesh in southern India," Dr. Kumar said. "He converted to Christianity as a young man but became no more touchable in the process. He then wore away his body piece by piece as a sharecropper—and I mean that literally: every day he would come home ever-so-slightly shorter, as if he walked on sandpaper instead of earth. By the time my father was born he'd lost two inches, by the time my father could read he'd lost five, by the time my father left for medical school it was eight, and when my father went home again to visit some years later just before taking a job in Iran, he found that his father was dead with nothing to dispose of: worn away to dust almost as if he'd been cremated by life. But I haven't told you, have I?, about my father yet.

"My father, Ramesh Moses Kumar, born three years before three bullets pierced the heart of our country's new Father, was determined to bring this heritage of grinding poverty to an end, and thanks to the Constitutional Mandate of 1950 on education, had a place to wear himself away doing so. He attended a new school in the mornings, worked alongside his father in the afternoons, and then went out after dark to the city's only lamppost to study through the night. 'The streets may be named Gandhi only,' he used to tell me, 'but the lampposts we should name for Maulana Azad.' That's independent India's first minister of education, you see, and one of my father's great heroes, what with his black fez like the top of a lamppost, and his unwavering commitment to free light.

119

"My father spent every night under the Maulana Azad Memorial Lamppost of the village of Panipatnam, as he called it, studying in the metaphorical presence of the recently-deceased minister he idolized, cramming square roots, textbook definitions, the Sanskrit and Latin names for this bone in that frog's leg into his young burning-with-ambition head until one night, smoke came out his ears and ascended to heaven like a ritual sacrifice. That's the night the angel came."

"Angel?" I said, "I'm sorry to interrupt your story, but hospitals are expected to be built on science, not religion, and I'm not sure how my insurance will feel about a doctor who anesthetizes using angels. Could you switch to something more realistic?"

"That's odd," a distant voice from the sky said. "You'd better hand me that retractor..."

Dr. Kumar sighed. "This is a true story," he said. "If you'd like, though, I can stop telling it and update you on your surgery instead."

"I'll take the angel," I told him.

"I'm glad," he said. "You know, angels really aren't that difficult to believe in if you see them as the dead, now glorified and doing the will of God. What else should the saints do after their violent deaths? This particular angel, it may interest you to know, had once lived a mortal life as the Apostle Thomas, who was cured of doubt forever by being sent to India, which is so vast that everything impossible has already happened at least twice. He died once in Gandhara, then again in Karnataka, then was sent back as an angel to watch over the Christians of his adopted country, a task which has kept him quite busy since.

"For example, as I was telling you, in 1959 he appeared beneath the glow of the Maulana Azad Memorial Lamppost of the village of Panipatnam to one Ramesh Moses Kumar, who would later become my father. Ramesh, who was preparing for his last exams in the public school and had been hampered on recent nights by persistent brownouts, didn't notice the angel at all at first, but said a quick prayer thanking God for the light, then closed his eyes and tried to remember the Latin name for a snake's kidney—until he heard the light say 'Moses!'

"A chill went down my father's back then in spite of the heat and humidity of the night. Then came the voice again 'Moses!' out of the lamp-light above and my father slowly began to raise his head until he could see, standing above him in the air, an angel descending in a pillar of fire from heaven, or possibly from some intermediate staging ground in the stratosphere. My father covered his face then and started to cry, which is, I suppose, the natural thing to do when you've never been descended upon by a pillar of fire before and then all at once—shoom!—it's upon you the night before your last and most significant publicly-funded exams, threatening to melt to a worthless metal lump the Maulana Azad Memorial Lamppost, which is the only local publicly-funded source of nighttime light available.

"All this should not have surprised the angel, who, after all, had nearly two millennia of experience, but for some reason, the whole twentieth century had proved rather disorienting for him, and so he paused for a moment before giving any comforting pronouncement, and my father simply sobbed into his book. The presence of a book, however, quickly reminded the angel what he had come for, and he spoke with a voice as radiant as his countenance and said to my father: 'Don't worry. You'll come in at the top of your class on exams.' That's when my father stopped crying and first really looked at him.

"'The Lord' said the angel of Saint Thomas, 'has seen your afflictions and sent me to bless you. As matter of fact,' he said, 'the Lord saw your affliction long before you were born and began arranging things even then. When the great Brahmin

Visak Anand's daughter grew alarmingly sick in 1895, the Lord sent Christian missionaries to his home to bless the girl. Out of gratitude for her life when she miraculously recovered, Anand declared that she would be raised a Christian and inherit one-half of all his wealth. And wouldn't you know that her granddaughter is about your age and that your pastor, even now, is mulling over how to ask her father if he'll offer her in marriage to a low-caste boy who shows great promise as a student, as, you know, a sort of scholarship to get him through medical school? And won't you be surprised when after ten, fifteen more years of work people are calling you Dr. Kumar? And in this way, the Lord will—

"But before the angel could tell my father what else the Lord was going to do, a growl that shook the dust up from the earth sounded in the not-so-distant darkness and my father saw there in the black the glint of terrible teeth and the dull sheen of venomous fingernails. A rakshasa, a Hindu demon, was lurking just past of edge of the light—and whether it was Maulana Azad's secular or the angel of Saint Thomas's religious light which kept him at bay, I do not know, but he still spoke into the space occupied by a light he was unwilling to touch.

"'Now wait just a minute,' the raskshasa said, 'along with each of your blessings, he ought to hear my curse. He is, after all, a traitor to the soil that gave birth to him, the son of a bastard father who took up the religion of a *firang*.'

"That's not a nice word, by the way," said Dr. Kumar. "I wouldn't use it if it weren't absolutely necessary to evoke the attitude of the demon."

"What does it mean?" I said.

"It's used to describe a person who arrives in a place where it's not felt that they belong" said Dr. Kumar.

"And the demon said this to your father?"

"He said it about my father's religion. As you can imagine, that upset the angel a great deal, and he began to grow sarcastic.

"'I had no idea you cared so much for a few dalits' said the angel.

"'It's a new age with a new politics' said the rakshasa.

"'New? I'm surprised one of your kind knows the meaning of that word.' said the angel.

"'Die again and go to hell this time' said the rakshas.

"'Can someone please tell me what is going on?' said my father, who bore both the Hindu name Ramesh and the Christian name Moses.

"'I bless you to become a doctor.' said the angel.

"'Ha! If that's your blessing, what is a curse?' said the rakshasa, 'If he wants to look at pus-filled wounds and contaminated stools all day, why should I stand in the way of that?'

"'I bless you to be married, as I've stated, to the great-granddaughter of Visak Anand,' said the angel.

"'That half-Tamil girl? So dark, how will he be able to find her in the night?' The rakshasa laughed and the stench of his breath reached the angel's feet, bringing back to him unpleasant memories of how it felt to be alive.

"'But that's not all—," said the angel, "you life's course will carry you far away from here to the land where Daniel the prophet once dwelt, a few kilometers east of where the Garden of Eden once grew.'

"'Now you're upsetting me,' said the rakshasa, 'if you want somewhere old and noble, try the Ganges or the isle of Lanka. I curse the lands of your book. When he goes there, may they be engulfed in war! May a bomb fall at his very feet!'

"'But I bless him,' said the angel, 'that the bomb won't harm him. And that when the curse comes true, he'll find his way out of there and eastward again.'

"Ha! Though he walks from one end of Iran to the other, wars will follow him. On the west side or the east, if he leaves this soil for that land, he'll be punished!'

"'I bless him to do God's work for the humble and oppressed, wherever his feet carry him.'

"'And I curse him with no paycheck! If a revolution itself has to get in the way, I'll see that he's not compensated.'

"'I bless him with children to care for him in his age.'

"'And I curse them with resentment toward him for forcing them all to be doctors! Let's see if they love pus-wounds and sniffing stools. Let's see if they love his short temper and angry lectures about grades.'

"'I bless his children to find strength in their faith.'

"'I curse them to join a lunatic sect that doesn't even let them drink chai!'

"With this, the rakshasa inched forward ever so slightly into the light. He rose to his full height of somewhere between three and five meters and howled: 'I curse him with the legacy of Brahmin and Britisher, of always thinking that light skin is better than dark. I curse him to care more for a prospective son-in-law's status and wealth than for his character. I curse him with a spirit of patriarchal autocracy. I curse him with an inability to ever step outside these early years' struggle and consider the feelings of someone else!'

"'I bless him,' the angel said, 'that when he is old, he will have a fig tree to care for, and that it will both occupy his hands and fill his heart.'

"And for that, the rakshasa had no answer, so he turned and fled back into the night. And the angel of Saint Thomas the Once-Doubter turned and looked down at my father, who, exhausted by the collected weight of years of study both behind and before him, had fallen asleep even before the angel and rakshasa had told him everything that was to come."

I vaguely remember waking up to a duller shade of pain than I'd known in more than a week. I celebrated this, naturally, by retching as thoroughly and exhaustingly as possible, trying to shake off the after-effects of that most unusual anesthetic I'd been given. Had the angelic light I'd witnessed been no more than the surgical lamp? Had the rakshasa been the surgeon himself, tearing into my body, carelessly leaving the toxins that would soon manifest themselves in a robust, hospital-strain staphylococcus infection?

"Uuuggghhhh?" I asked the first time I heard a nurse come in to check my vitals.

"That bad?" said the nurse.

"Where's Dr. Kumar?" I said, trying my best not to sound desperate.

"Kumar?" said the nurse.

"Junior. I have to see Dr. Kumar, Junior" I said. The nurse glanced over some papers.

"I'm not quite sure who you're talking about" said the nurse.

"In anesthesiology. Looks Indian," I said, "it's not that complicated!"

"Sir, half the doctors in this hospital look Indian," said the nurse. "Can I get you another pillow or something to drink?"

It is at moments like this when I often remind myself to breathe deeply. By breathing deeply, one can avoid many unpleasant and embarrassing experiences. Such as, for instance, berating an overworked nurse for failing to know the younger Doctor Kumar. Or, to take the example a step further, attempting to use one's IV to pull down the bag-carrying metal rack onto an unsuspecting nurse's head. If one is to persuade a nurse to take time out of his busy work schedule in order to look up the phone number of a certain anesthesiologist, one must use any respiratory technique available in order to see beyond such options and establish a relationship of trust. Or so

I reasoned. Unfortunately, however, attempting to breathe deeply while intensely nauseated can also lead to such mishaps as, say, a fit of vomiting out of an already impoverished stomach which contains, let us imagine, only acids, and onto an overworked nurse.

The nurse did not get me a pillow or a drink. When I asked again about Dr. Kumar, he left for some time. I was probably either asleep or delirious when he returned.

In my dreams, bombs are falling on the street between the hospital and a mosque. A middle-aged Dr. Kumar Sr. walks to work with an umbrella. The umbrella is incredible—it is painted in pure whites, bold saffrons, deep greens: colors which are, for a bomb-filled street between a mosque and a hospital, rather abrupt, rakish, even—shall I say it?—*gaudy*. It is an umbrella that I, for one, would never have the courage, self-assurance, or brashness to carry. Perhaps the doctor has none of these. Perhaps the doctor is simply oblivious. Perhaps the doctor is too absorbed in his work to notice what umbrella he is carrying, or even how the bombs, aimed (as if by some curse) toward his head bounce casually off of it and go careening off hundreds of feet to explode in dark alleys.

My envy for these bombs must be acknowledged. They are launched by hands that value them more than life, they shine in their Icaresque ascents, they dive with a self-consuming passion towards their destination, which is (conveniently) also their destiny—and then, and this is what wrenches my guts—they hit the umbrella, it destroys their perfect arcs and rational plans, it sends them spinning off at unexpected angles on unplanned odysseys and instead of falling apart, like any reasonable person would, at the life-breaking interruption, they flip like happy dolphins, they rush off athletically to the *wrong deaths*. How do they manage this with such fatalistic grace?

Dr. Kumar Sr. stops, stoops, picks up a newspaper which has been discarded on the street. A bomb falls, bounces of his garish umbrella, glints—I swear—as if to wink at me. It flies rapidly upwards again, mistakes my window for the sky. Showering glass shards across my body like confetti, it bursts into my room. The heat radiates off its body and it pauses for a moment like some Kabuki actor above me in the air. A mechanical voice in my memory tells me to "Breathe in. Hold—your breath." A moment passes. The MRI machine's voice says "Breathe" and the bomb explodes, though I'm blinded too quickly to appreciate the finer points of its pyrotechnical culmination.

`Your father`
—I began to write, after I noticed that I was awake, in a note to be delivered to Dr. Kumar, Junior—
`once worked, according to the angel of Saint Thomas, near the Garden of Eden. I am not a religious man, but my grandmother firmly believed the Garden of Eden to be the original site of the invention of death, so I can see why your doctor-father would have been asked to work so near to there. Assuming, of course, that your` ~~`doctor has a father`~~ `father is a doctor. I'm not sure whether I know that. I remember you telling me, but I might have been seeing things at the time. You see, I'm having difficulty establishing what's real and what's not real, what I know and what I don't know, what matters and what doesn't matter, and whether any of those mean the same thing.`
`Doctor.`
—I wrote—
`You have to help me. The anesthetic has gone wrong. Or else I have reason to believe that the cancer has spread to my brain. Or else I am delirious and fevered and seeing visions of your`

father crossing the street in a city where bombs
fall like rain.
    P.S. The nurse is not helpful and doesn't even
know who you are. Please come quickly.
    —I tried to read over the note once more to see what I'd
forgotten, but focusing on the words hurt my eyes. Terrible,
isn't it, never to be sure just what you've said?

"There are two Doctor Kumars in anesthesiology" said the
nurse, who had a disconcerting Cheshire-Catly habit of
appearing and disappearing without warning, "Dr. Satish
Kumar and Dr. John Kumar—neither with a junior. I didn't see
either name on your chart, but you seemed to know what you
were talking about." He handed me a slip of paper with their
phone extensions before checking my catheter.
    My face flushed. "That's very kind of you" I said, ashamed
of having committed to writing my impression of his
uselessness.
    "You're welcome" said the nurse, "but it's really not that
difficult. The urine is all encased in plastic."
    "For the phone numbers" I said.
    "Oh. Sure thing" said the nurse. I watched him swap out
my old drainage bag for a fresh new one, and marveled for the
first time at my easy access to such useful resources.
    "You're right about the bags, though," I said, "amazing
technology."
    "Oh?" said the nurse.
    "Crude oil into plastic. It's better than water into wine" I
said.
    "I'd never thought of it like that" said the nurse.
    "Neither had I!" I said, "To think I'm kept clean by
something which was once thick and black and spewing out
from beneath the earth in a place like Iraq or Iran—it's
magnificent!" I laughed then, long and hard—or at least until

my throat, eyes, and sinuses ached from the exertion. Is it possible that even after my own laughter had receded, I could still hear a sickly, cough-smeared echo of my laugh coming from beneath my bed? I looked up to alert the nurse, but true his Cheshire-Catly ways, the nurse had already somehow gone away. I lay alone, or perhaps only almost alone, in the darkness, wondering what the laugh-echo I thought I'd heard might promise or threaten.

That's when I felt the claws piercing the sides of my chest.

In my dreams, Dr. Ramesh Moses Kumar is walking across the same street as before when a bomb falls—plunk!—at his feet, having missed the protective umbrella by mere inches. In this instant, Dr. Kumar's obliviousness is demolished, and though the bomb is a total dud, ignition-wise, and just lies on the ground in an impotent heap, I can tell that in his mind, Dr. Kumar Sr. has been killed by this bomb already once and will be again the next hundred times he closes his eyes. So Dr. Kumar decides not to sleep. He and his wife each pack one bag that night, leave a big case of their belongings with a local nurse-friend, and walk away from the sunset, feet trudging all night in the direction of the coming morning, eyes straining to stay awake until they're safely away from that city where bombs rain down from the sky, which lies just east of the border where men stand in line at the gates of hell and paradise.

How strange that in my dreams, the Doctor strains so hard to stay awake! I can't recall if it was that juxtaposition or the insistent and abnormal beeping of the machine I was connected to which jarred me awake.

The doctors and nurses ran as if the bombs had spilled into the hospital from the street of my dreams. And maybe they had, maybe this explained the burning sensation I felt, maybe this and not a monster under the bed explained the clutching pains on the inside of my chest.

If you were to ask which doctor's advice of another surgery I responded to, I'd have to make an uneducated guess. If you wished to know what permissions I gave and which forms I signed, I'd draw a blank.

I remember most clearly that, as they wheeled me in for surgery once again, I caught a glimpse of Dr. John Kumar. He didn't ask me to count, simply slipped some solution into my saline and watched electronic signals for signs of my life or the approach of some angel of death. I wanted to speak to him, to ask him about what happened to his father, but couldn't find my voice or any words.

When I was a child, my grandfather's wartime years were smothered in silence. This is, I think, what happens to most people who serve in foreign wars: the languages of *there* and of *here* are so different as to baffle the would-be translator mute. Take, for example, the syntax of pain: in the grammar of *there*, it is invariably rendered as an exclamation, whereas in the grammar of *here*, it is most often formulated as a question. How, then, to speak of such a devious shape-shifter?

From my grandmother, I learned about pain as manifested in an old and decaying Bible picture book: David, bearing Goliath's severed head. Sampson, blinded by Delilah but praying to find strength for one last act of terrorism. Jesus, arriving at last on a cross he'd been carrying for three years. But where were those pictures when I needed them? Where were the old yellowed pages I could point at like a pain chart to tell the Doctor: "tell me a story, because it hurts like this"?

My uncle used to set out to visit foreign countries, only to arrive somewhere in their pasts. When I asked him for bedtime stories, he would tell me about real atrocities. "We live" he'd say, "but we don't learn, at least not very much and never for too long. And so we're always gambling against cruelty at losing long-term odds." And then he'd leave me to lie alone in the still darkness, where I'd imagine dice that summoned Leopold's men on a one, revived Hitler on a two, started a Cultural Revolution on a three, brought Pinochet north to our country on a four, brought a plague on a five, and killed your grandparents and uncle on a six.

Long before I was old enough to develop any perspective on pain, of course, my parents were both dead.

"One" I said, and Dr. Kumar looked down at me, surprised.

"Two," I said, "Three. Four. Five."

I opened my eyes "Tell me a story about your father," I said.

"No," said Dr. Kumar Jr. "I don't like to think too much about him. I'm sorry you had to see him in the first place."

"Please" I said, "please, just tell me another story."

"Shall I tell you about the way he used to treat our mother? Shall I tell you about the time he tried to arrange a marriage for my sister with a man whose only qualification was an MD, who turned out to be an alcoholic who abused his own parents? Is that what you want to hear? Or would you rather hear about what he expected of me, demanded of me? Is that what you're fishing for?"

"You do resent him, then, just like the demon predicted you would?"

"There is no demon. I made that up to keep you doped up for the surgery. I made everything up: the angel, the demon, the vision, Maulana Azad, everything. None of them exist!"

"The Lamppost?"

"Well, OK, that part is true. You saw it with your own eyes. I have a father and he studied under a lamppost long ago in a space and time very much unlike now and here."

"Did he go to Iran?"

Silence. Doctor John Kumar said nothing for a while. "Why are you so interested in this?"

Silence. I said nothing for a while. "I keep dreaming about him there."

"Maybe Iran doesn't exist. Maybe I made that part up, too. Or maybe he made up one Iran only to arrive in another. And maybe that other Iran was made up, too, and was therefore overthrown by a third Iran, at once as real and fictitious as the rest."

"Did he go Iran?"

"No."

"I saw him there. I saw the bombs."

"Then yes, he went and worked willingly but then there was a revolution and soon he was too trapped to visit us in India and so raised us over the telephone."

"You and your sister didn't go with him?"

"Of course not, no."

"But your mother—she was with him, they were walking eastward across the country. Did they leave you alone?"

"We were with family. We were alone. I made Iran up and they were in India with us the whole time. What does it matter to you?"

I closed my eyes. "I have to know" I said, "what happened to your father when they got east. I have to know," I said, right about to cry, "whether your father ever escaped."

"No," said John Kumar, "and yes. And also no." He sighed. "All right, I'll tell you a story."

"Where to begin? Or rather, where to proceed from where I once before bagan? Let's start with this: my father, as you know, married my mother and was thus able to afford medical school, but thanks to persistent discrimination, struggled at first to find work—until a missionary doctor at a leprosy hospital prayed to God to send him aid in the form of a young, native, Christian doctor on the day before my father applied.

"My father worked for wages dictated by the limitations of charity work and a theology of self-sacrifice, and shouldn't have been as surprised as he was to discover that some members of the staff were robbing the hospital blind. But oh, his righteous anger ran hot, and oh, how he rebuked those men for their corruption, and oh, how he awakened the old missionary to the hospital's plight, and together they cleansed that hospital like Jesus cleansing the temple, which is how, I think, my father came to believe so firmly in Progress, despite all the subsequent evidence.

"After my sister and I were born, of course, charity wages wouldn't do, but my father left his post for the siren-call of a far-off Shah who promised good money and golden pensions to Indian MD émigrés with the feeling that, in his own small way, he'd improved the world at that missionary hospital, which of course he had.

"But how does the hope of local improvement hold up against systemic collapse? In Iran, as you know, he had to teach himself to ignore the Revolution, then the Iran-Iraq war, until a bomb fell at his feet and he decided to leave his post and run. All across Iran he and my mother walked. When they were caught, they would work because no one wished to return a doctor they could use for discipline or punishment. He was like a human coin, found and spent a dozen times: don't watch it, though, and it goes wandering. Whenever the opportunity presented itself, my parents would head eastwards again, toward India. Bharat. Hindustan. Home.

"They arrived at last, penniless, at Iran's eastern borders and were fortunate to find a gurdwara were they were allowed to sleep and eat for free. Their Sikh hosts even offered them soap and water with which to wash before presenting themselves at the pre-1947 borders of the land they called home.

"At the border, however, they were informed that for an Indian doctor and his wife to pass through Pakistan was impossible. So my father sat and watched Baluchi drug smugglers crossing the border this way and that, trying to imagine how to smuggle himself and his wife home under their vests, but he knew such hopes were vain, and so he and my mother walked again northward until the Pakistan border was out of sight.

"He had hoped to reach Mashhad, and perhaps find some peace in that city of ancient martyrs, but my father had walked too much in step with the pace of war: no sooner had he been caught and put to work in a local hospital in southeastern Khorasan than Afghan refugees from the Soviet invasion began pouring into Iran by the hundred-thousands. The local military commander took my grandfather to their camps, asked him to single-handedly heal their cramped and dirty populations.

"In one camp, there was an outbreak of cholera. Can you imagine? Thousands of people quarantined into a few square miles, in which there is nowhere to wash one's hands and the sick are losing gallons of their bodies' water to diarrhea every day. Infected fluids spill unchecked over the cots and the ground. Excrement and disease tinge all the water everyone has to drink. And one doctor should fix all this?

"My father told the commander that under these conditions, everyone in the camp would die. The commander told my father that a doctor could prescribe medicines, but not a new camp. My father asked if some of the uninfected could be moved out of the camp; the commander said no. Then my father filled up with the old righteous anger again and said to the commander: 'All these people will die here and God will hold you responsible for their deaths!' The officer grew indignant, said 'What can I do? Is this war my fault?' My father said: 'Close the camp and send these people back to Afghanistan. If they die there, God will look to that country for the responsibility.' And so it was that the commander closed the camp, freeing the people from certain death in Iran, leaving them to probable death in their Soviet-occupied homeland.'

"This incident, this compromised victory, proved to be my father's greatest wartime triumph. His courage and dedication awed his Iranian colleagues such that when a different disease invaded my father's own body some years later, when it set up an occupation which could not easily be expelled, they intervened on his behalf for an early retirement and two plane tickets home. His Shah-promised pension, of course, never followed him."

"I'd like to ask your father," I said, "how to find dignity in a world which makes so little sense."

"He tends a fig tree" John Kumar said, "in California, in my sister's backyard."

When I woke up again in my own hospital bed, I immediately searched for the scrap of paper the nurse had brought me. I found it near the telephone and left a message for Doctor John Kumar, saying "Do you exist?" and "Were you present at my surgeries last week and last night?"   When the nurse came, I asked him to check for a monster under my bed, perhaps an aging Hindu demon with an oddly comforting sarcastic streak? The nurse laughed, apparently under the impression that I was joking. As he changed my bedpan, I thought of the camp full of cholera. How long, oh Lord of Dr. Kumar's father, must such suffering go on?

"Thank you" I told the nurse as a way of clearing my mind.

"For what?" he said.

"For nothing in particular," I said, "I just feel like I should thank someone."

Doctor Kumar called back to confirm that he'd been the anesthesiologist for my surgeries, but said he'd had trouble understanding my other question and what was it I wanted to know?

The trouble with asking a person whether he or she exists is that during any given conversation, the answer always seems self-evident: it's only later, with the murkiness of hindsight, that doubt sets in. So I told Dr. Kumar I wanted to discuss some side-effects I might have had from the anesthesia and asked if it's normal for a patient to stay awake through the ten count and for most of the surgery and yet not remember seeing anything that went on.

"I'm not sure" said Dr. Kumar "as far as I could tell, in that first surgery you were out by two."

"Do you drink tea?" I said.

"No," said Dr. Kumar.

"And for you, that's a matter of religious faith?"

"Yes. Have you known other Latter-day Saints, then?"

"Was your father a doctor?" I said.

"Yes" said John Kumar.

"And he encouraged you to become a doctor?" I said.

He hesitated. "You could put it that way."

"You've been thinking about him a great deal lately?"

"I suppose I have...yes" said John Kumar. "Yes, definitely. Why are you asking this?"

"He lived in Iran once and in California now?"

"Yes...you know him, then?" said John Kumar.

"I don't think so" I said. "Not quite, in any case. I don't understand him yet."

John Kumar laughed. "Of course you don't. Neither do I."

My desk is, presumably, still cluttered with papers which, in the not-so-distant past, I found extremely important. My car, I suppose, is still in need of changed oil.

I lie in a hospital room and stare at the ceiling, remembering things my uncle once told me about the brutal reign of Leopold II over Congo. I consider my own position and wonder how exactly the hierarchies of pain and fear operate, wonder where my own suffering currently falls among the hundred billion or so people who have ever lived on the earth. I remember the bright teeth and matted hair of the rakshasa I saw under anesthesia that first night of the current phase of my life. Is the rakshasa also the weakened, rasping monster who lies under my bed, who graces me with the occasional embrace? It's so difficult to be certain of anything in this world!

I had a sweet dream last night. I saw the fig tree Dr. Kumar Sr. tends in his daughter's backyard. He visits it even more faithfully than he once visited the Maulana Azad Memorial Lamppost of Panipatnam. The retired doctor tends the tree with a tenderness I would not have anticipated.

I do not know, for certain, whether he does so because the tree actually bears figs or simply because he loves the way that the sprouting leaves remind one, as Jesus says in the Bible, of the promise of a coming summer.

Acknowledgments

Nicole Wilkes Goldberg—for her editorial vision and for coming to the rescue when I was locked in a tower

Mattathias Singh Goldberg Westwood—for bugging me to make 2019 a "year of Goldberg" and finally get this and other collections in print

The writing group variously known as the Seizure Ninjas, Johnny Hollis School of Illegal Teenage Driving, and Accidental Erotica (featuring Janci Patterson, Megan Walker, Lee Ann Setzer, Heather Clark, Christopher Husberg, Jenn Johansson, Heidi Summers Creer, Ruth Owen, and Mike Barbeau)—for feedback, encouragement, and a place to talk shop

Bapuji and Grandma Gill—for supporting me while I learned this craft and explored these worlds

Ramesh Moses Murala and Daisy Salvam—for sharing stories and making memories

Orson Scott Card and the 2012 Literary Boot Camp group—for bringing me to Greensboro and helping me shape a story there

Prick of the Spindle and *Mormon Artist*—for giving Maulana Azad and Teancum Singh Rosenberg homes in their pages

And of course, the old Hostess Brands Company—for inspiring "The Trial of al-Mansur"

About the Author

James Goldberg's family is Jewish on one side, Sikh on the other, and Mormon in the middle. He is the only person to have won the Association for Mormon Letters Award for both Drama (*Prodigal Son,* 2008) and Novel (*The Five Books of Jesus,* 2012). He is a co-founder, with Nicole Wilkes Goldberg and Scott Hales, of the annual Mormon Lit Blitz writing contest and currently writes for the Church of Jesus Christ of Latter-day Saints' History Department.

Also by James Goldberg

The Five Books of Jesus

It starts in the desert. John the prophet lowers Jesus under the Jordan's muddy waters and pulls him up, just as a bird swoops down to skim the river's surface. It spreads next to Galilee, where some welcome Jesus as a disciple of John and others grow wary of his rising influence—fishermen are leaving their nets, tax collectors their offices, and students their masters to listen to this new saint. After abandoning his nets, Andrew ties knots in the threads of his shirt to remember Jesus' teachings. After escaping his slum, Judas waits for Jesus to call down the legions of angels who can end a broken world. But just as Jesus' movement in the north is gaining strength, he turns south toward the Temple and a fate his followers will struggle to understand. *The Five Books of Jesus*, James Goldberg's lyrical novelization of Jesus' ministry, tells the story of the gospels as Jesus' followers might have experienced it: without knowing what would happen next or how to make sense of events as they unfold.

Let Me Drown with Moses

The forty-nine poems in *Let Me Drown with Moses* are not for those who think of religion as another name for self-help. They are for those who still believe in a God who wrestles. For those who think faith should challenge as much as it comforts. For those who would follow a prophet chest-deep into the Red Sea, even before the waters part.
Drawing on imagery from scripture and Mormon history, *Let Me Drown With Moses* gives voice to the spiritual longing of a people and does its own small part to keep religion a living language in the 21st century.

Phoenix Song

In this follow-up to his 2015 collection, *Let Me Drown with Moses*, James Goldberg explores themes of suffering, community, faith, and discipleship with both an unflinching commitment to God and a clear-eyed perspective on the difficulties of mortality. Whether telling stories from Goldberg's LDS ward, chronicling his experience in chemotherapy, imagining alternate histories, or commenting on the scriptures and society, the poems in Phoenix Song describe what it means both to feel burned to the ground and to rise from the ashes.

Remember the Revolution: Mormon Essays and Stories

In 2006, 22-year-old James Goldberg moved to Utah, dreaming of possibilities for Mormon artistic community. Though the ride was often rough, he spent the next five years feeling his way forward, finding a voice to speak the language of the tradition in his own distinct register. The twelve essays and short stories in *Remember the Revolution* chronicle those experiments, giving voice to the idealism, anxiety, and insight of a young Mormon writer.

Whether imagining the experience of a Mormon Bollywood playback singer, giving the German Jewish philosopher Walter Benjamin a seat in Primary, telling the story of the early Restoration through an imagined sequence of Joseph Smith's anxious dreams, or writing an inverted theology in the form of spam emails, Goldberg grapples with ways Mormon thought can engage with the cultures around it and speak to the pressing questions simmering beneath the surface of the modern world. At turns sincere, satirical, surreal, and somber, *Remember the Revolution* is vital reading for anyone interested in the potential of a distinctly Mormon literature.

CPSIA information can be obtained
at www.ICGtesting.com
Printed in the USA
LVHW041138111119
636960LV00004B/1449